This is Where I Leave You

First Published in the UK in 2013 as
Crossing Life Lines

Other books by Rachel Dove

The Chic Boutique on Baker Street
The Flower Shop on Foxley Street
The Wedding Shop on Wexley Street
The Fire House on Honeysuckle Street

The Long Walk Back

Nice Guys Finish Lonely
Summer Hates Christmas

For my family, who always believed I could finish this book,

To my husband, who suffered while I was writing it

And to my children, who are my everything.

CHAPTER 1

As the box was lowered into the ground Cady wanted to scream. Scream and jump into the gaping hole and cry like an infant. The man in the coffin was gone forever. She felt cheated.

Cheated out of the final showdown; cheated out of mowing down the philandering bastard herself. Stupid taxi. The white hot rage in the pit of her stomach snarled and wailed. It was all she could do not to rip off the coffin lid and poke his dead eyes out with her fingers.

She raised her head and looked around at the sea of mourners dressed in black standing around the graveside. Was **she** here? Or was she watching from a distance? Did she really have the balls to stand here and weep? There were plenty of wailing women here; many from his office; it could be anyone of them. Cady glanced at her mother-in-law who was crying and shaking. She never did cut those apron strings. Not that Richard ever wanted to, it had always surprised Cady that he still did not suckle on her when she visited, which was often. A sketch from Little Britain popped into her head. David Walliams as a suit type taking his girlfriend to meet the folks for the first time and then breastfeeding on his mum. 'Bitty, bitty!'

A laugh burbled in her chest and Cady choked it down, turning it into a muffled sob, or what she hoped sounded like one. Georgina squeezed her hand. Cady looked at her best friend and knew she felt her pain, anger and rage.
The mourners gradually moved away, muttering and sniffing, to the cars that would deliver them to the wake. Georgina and Cady stood there till they were alone with Richard. The breeze ruffled the plastic wrappings and ribbons around the flowers. The big motionless wooden box stuffed in the ground looked at odds to the surroundings, all bending and yielding to the wind. It was surreal; actually, surreal was a great word to describe her life at present.

Surreal. Cady would laugh again if she didn't think it would wrench apart her chest and leave her in a bloody heap.
"You coming, or want me to wait in the car?" Georgina said tactfully.
"No, I'm coming. Let's just get this over with."
"Cady, I..'
"NO! I am done Georgina, let's go."
Georgina nodded and headed to the car. Cady glanced at the coffin in the ground, turned on her heel and strode away.

The wake was a pretentious affair. Richard, the organised soul that he was, had planned his own funeral and stipulated his desires right down to the caterers and golf club setting. He had left it with his will he had devised with his father, Richard senior, head partner at Everett and Stokes. Cady had been only too glad to let him and his mother deal with the arrangements. His mother thought it was grief she was suffering, but what Cady really felt more was an acute nothingness. It was like going to the dentist, that numb, tingling around the edges feeling you get just before you go under; except the numbness had lasted for days. Cady had not been home since it happened; she couldn't face it. Georgina had kindly put her up, and brought her some clothes and bits she needed the night it happened…ugh, she could not even think about that.

So here she was, sat in a black dress Georgina had picked up for her in Debenhams, staring at a lot of people milling around, quaffing champagne and triangles of cucumber sandwiches, while a harpist played in the corner of the room. It reeked of Richard and his family. Cady could have walked in naked and no-one would have noticed. She was just the wife after all, the secretary who 'married up.' Fucked herself up more like. Now she was a 29 year old widow with an empty, soulless house full of crap, a job in the firm he worked for; and a clinic appointment the following Tuesday to check if the son of a bitch hadn't left her with a nasty parting gift from his skanky hook ups. To say that turning 30 was a bone crunching, gut wrenching thought was the understatement of eternity.
Cady's dull senses picked up a soft tinkle of laughter. Looking towards the noise she saw Angela. She was laughing and joking

with Richard's mother, Priscilla. Angela was a blonde leggy Amazon. A solicitor in his firm, and a high flier by all accounts; with her Gucci handbags, kick ass court records and cocktails after work. Angela flicked her honey highlighted long hair over her elegant figure hugging black dress, let out another soft ripple of laughter and stroked Priscilla's arm warmly. Cady headed over.
"I know darling, but I really do think that Richard would have made you a lovely husband, it's such a tragedy, it really is, and now my only child has gone and I will never have a grandchild to look forward…oh, h-hello Cady dear, I wondered where you had gotten to, have you eaten? You look pale…"
Cady stared at Priscilla, scarcely believing her own ears. How dare she try to set up her son posthumously with another woman! And grandchildren, what a joke! Richard never wanted children! Cady herself had tried for years to get him to have a family with her. Now what? Priscilla just brushed her son's wife under the carpet on the day of his funeral? What was she supposed to do, shuffle off quietly and start knitting cardigans and rescuing flea bitten moggies? Start erecting her Richard shrine?
Cady stood up straight, and pushing out her boobs and her British stiff upper lip, coolly eyed Angela.
"Why hello Angela, lovely of you to come. Such a tragedy yes, for dear Richard to die so young, shame you never knew each other better, I agree! How AWFUL!"
She was aware that she was raising her voice and practically shouting now, but she didn't care anymore. How fucking dare Priscilla! She glanced around at the posh strangers; their hands stuck midway between shovelling more sandwiches down their snotty, elitist mouths. Georgina caught her eye and was edging towards the emerging ugly scene, pleading with her eyes for Cady to hold it in and get through it - but it was too late for that.
Priscilla, rotund and sweating in her dark garb, placed her hand on Cady's shoulder. "Ah…dear, I was just saying, that's all, it's such a waste and I miss him so much, a...as, I am sure you do, it's just…"
"Well, all is not lost, dear Priscilla, maybe we could go and dig him up and Angela can have a crack at him, eh? Plenty to talk about, I've no doubt, degrees and Tort, that kind of thing, yes?"

Angela's eyes widened and Priscilla's mouth dropped. A collective nasal gasp reverberated round the room. The harpist had even stopped playing. Cady felt hot and sweaty and angry. She realised she'd gone too far and there was only one way to go now.
Priscilla rallied, exclaiming, "Cady, I can't believe your behaviour, at your own husband's funeral! Are you drunk?"
Cady was stone cold sober and felt more alive than she had in years.
She laughed bitterly and spat back at her mother-in law, "No, Priscilla dear, I am not drunk, but I soon will be! You've never accepted me; you've belittled me and sidestepped me all my married life - and one good thing to come out of all this is that we will never have to cross paths again!"
Cady turned and headed for the French doors next to the bar area. She needed to get outside; the air in here was choking her and she could feel sweat running down her back onto her dress, her rage and disgust potent and bubbling within her veins. The incredible hulk would have done a double take crossing paths with her today. She heard the crowd murmur comments of disgust and discreet enjoyment, and Priscilla called after her, "Cady, you get back here, you silly young girl, you can't disrespect me like this!" Cady turned and eyed her, steel rods shooting out of her eyes and poking Priscilla in her fat sausage like body.
"Oh and by the way, dear mother-in-law, your chances of a grandchild are not completely dashed yet, your precious son was shagging half of the office, so maybe a precious little bastard will pop up for you soon eh? Chin up!"
And clattering away on her heels, Cady hooked a bottle of champers under each arm from the drinks table and high kicked the French doors open, striding across the lawn every inch the elegant, grieving widow.

CHAPTER 2

Georgina snapped her phone shut and sighed in frustration, puffing her ultra modern fringe off her face with her irritated, shaking with rage breath. She glanced at her Cartier watch and groaned. Her flight was due to leave for Paris in ten minutes and she couldn't get hold of Cady. Her bed had not been slept in when she checked this morning at her apartment, and her mobile was switched off. No-one was answering at the house she had shared with Richard, although she could not imagine that she had slept there, she hadn't set foot near the place since that night. *Jesus, Cady, where are you?*

Georgina glared at her phone, willing it to ring. Then the tannoy announced the last call for her flight. Georgina pushed down the sick feeling in her stomach and smoothing her smart skirt suit over her lithe, tanned legs, picked up her suitcase and click clacked to the gate, every step in her Louboutins taking her further away from her distraught friend. Man, this business trip was going to be a killer, she thought. Cady had better be ok.

Pulling out her passport from her oversized Louis Vuitton handbag, her eyes were drawn to the file containing the details of the business contact she was due to meet in France; the predictable type with family money and a corporate job in daddy's business with money to burn. And nothing between the ears but Cristal and Ferraris.

Should be a breeze, but why did she not feel excited like normal at the prospect? The high flying job, expense account, great apartment? Any woman would kill to be in her position. Maybe it was just leaving Cady like this. The two friends had been inseparable since they were seven years old and Georgina had moved in with her aunt when her parents had moved to America for their high flying careers, leaving their only daughter behind. They felt it was best to keep her in England, and not disrupt her education or rip her away from her friends and everything familiar at home. Georgina soon realised though, that she was seen as more of an inconvenience to their careers and wining dining lifestyles, and the trips to the States to visit her folks soon became few and far between, firstly due to her parents' constant excuses and cancellations, and lastly due to Georgina simply refusing to go. Not that her mother or father ever pushed the subject. Georgina could sense their relief each time; now when she spoke to them, it was usually short and sweet and she could hear the happiness in their voices at their corporate, plush, child free life.

They still sent her money every month, but Georgina was making so much from her own job that she never touched it; it just languished in her HISA. The thought of using the money never occurred to her. She saw it as buy off money and would rather have been a poor child than a latch key one. Her Aunt had brought her up well and they were still close, but she had always felt the loss of her parents throughout her teen years. Still, it had taught her the power of total independence, and the importance of never relying on anyone or letting someone into her life. Well, except Cady.

What was Cady going to do now? If Richard wasn't already dead she would bloody ring his neck herself.

Handing her passport to the perky flight attendant at the gate she smiled to herself at the flight attendant's obvious jealousy at her expensive clothes and immaculately turned out appearance. She boarded the plane, settled into her seat and buried her head into the contact file for the rest of the flight.

CHAPTER 3

Opening a crusty, puffed up eye, Cady peeked at her surroundings and winced at the pain that shot through her skull upon contact with the sunlight to her eyeball. Ugh. Mouth like sandpaper, check. Brain too big for shaky, dried out head, check. Dry, salty tongue, check.
She gingerly opened her other eye and scanned her surroundings with a fear of dread. The Moet champagne bottles lay on their side on the floor, empty. She was laid on her sofa at home and still wearing her funeral clothes. The TV flickered in the corner, showing the title screen for Bridget Jones's Diary. Ah. She remembered now. She had come home to the home she shared with Richard, got raucously, rip roaringly drunk, ate her own body weight in crisps and chocolate, and watched Bridget Jones - twice. The first time screaming at Daniel whilst throwing snacks at his smug, philandering face. And the second time, crying her eyes out, thinking how much she and Bridget were like each other; both fumbling through life encountering fuckwits while everyone else seemed to flow through it smugly. Where was her Darcy? In her Austenesque brain, years ago, she thought she had found him in Richard. How laughingly wrong that thought was.

Today was the reading of Richard's Will. She shuddered at the thought of sitting in a room with Richard's nearest and dearest after her outburst yesterday. She had not even considered his Will, not until now. What if Richard put something in there about his fancy piece? She couldn't bear the thought of people pitying her; laughing up their sleeves at the silly secretary who was sharing her husband with half of the legal quarter of Wakefield. Work was another thing she would have to get her head round as well. She couldn't stay off forever. It had only been a week of course, and no-one would expect her to be back at her desk yet, but she had to return sometime. She was alone now and would need the money more than ever.
She dragged her tired, hung-over body off the overstuffed, manly couch (Richard's choice). She traversed the room like a newborn giraffe, and clinging to the banister, made her way to the bathroom.

The meeting was at 10am and it was 8.56am already. She’d take a cab; she’d be way over the limit and not fit to drive.

CHAPTER 4

Grinding to a halt outside the small row of neat houses, Luke Masters rested his push bike against the brick wall and reached into his battered rucksack for some flyers. The area was nice here, nicer than in town where he lived in a riverside apartment. He liked his apartment, but it was essentially a tiny box within a tower of tiny boxes, and the rent was huge. Wakefield was trying to move with the times, and the result was tiny apartments at huge rents. Still, a bonus of living where he did was that he could see the Hepworth Gallery out of his living room window. He loved that space. It was his second home; the muse for his inspiration. Being an artist himself, albeit a struggling one, he really needed the inspiration, and the cash. Hence today's visit and dropping leaflets through doors to advertise his painting and decorating, jack-of-all trades services. He could turn his hand to anything, his dad Jack was a practical sort, running his own building firm, and had taught him well. His mother Arabella was the arty-farty type, as dad called her, the creative one; the one who could make a doily out of a piece of string whilst simultaneously knocking up a pineapple upside-down cake and painting her toe nails.
It was his mother's creative independent streak that had him delivering flyers today, his dad was always offering him work at his firm, and although he loved working alongside his dad, he got more thrills and job satisfaction from drumming up his own little paid jobs and seeing them through to completion. The artist in him loved the painting and decorating too, even if it was just a touch of emulsion and glossing a few dado rails.

As he walked up to number 3, he noticed that the curtains were almost completely drawn shut and there were a number of cards on the bare windowsill. Hmm, bet it was someone's birthday, he thought, the occupants are probably still in bed pissed.
As he pushed the folded leaflet into the letterbox slot, the door opened roughly, taking half of his finger skin with it.
"JESUS CHRIST! FU...!"

Luke's profanity died in his throat. The woman opening the door was staring at him with a mad expression on her face, eyebrow arched, lips pulled back in a 'who the hell are you' grimace. She was dressed smartly in a simple grey suit, white shirt and red handbag, but she looked tired and drawn. Her blue eyes still had smudged mascara flecks around the edges and her blonde highlighted hair was scraped back into a loose, messy chignon. Glancing down her body, he saw long tight clad pins encased in a pair of nude kitten heels. Nice legs too….

"Er hum, can I help you?"

Luke realised he had been staring at her agog and checking her legs out for what seemed the last five minutes.

He closed his mouth and concentrated on his pitch.

"Hi, yes, er Luke, I mean, I am Luke, sorry, I was just popping this flyer through your door, I am a handyman service you see, can do anything, painting, DIY, my dad is in the building business too, so basically we can do anything between us, big or small so.."

He proffered the flyer. Taking it and glancing at her watch, she smiled thinly. Luke could smell the feminine scent of Davidoff Cool Water, and a not so feminine waft of stale alcohol, and… could he smell cheese?

"I will bear it in mind, Liam, thanks. Not to be rude, but I have to go…."

Stuffing the flyer into her pocket, she turned on her heels and headed to the waiting cab that Luke had not heard arrive.

Luke realised he was staring after the car as it drove out of sight. Wow, she must have had one hell of a birthday party….

Sighing and physically shaking his head to dislodge the memory of those legs, he carried on up the street. He would certainly have something to tell his dad tonight over mum's shepherd's pie.

CHAPTER 5

Richard was apoplectic with rage. Dead, how could he be bloody dead!? He didn't have the time to be dead! What the hell was going on? Wiped out by a taxi on the way back to the office he practically lived at had to be the lamest death ever. Richard was embarrassed. Which is strange, because should he not be feeling something else, sadness, pain, grief? He actually felt pissed off. Pissed off, yet eerily calm and detached from the actual event of his death…as though he were watching it happen to somebody else. He was seriously annoyed that he had gone at this time. He had a new life beckoning. He had so much work to do, Cady to deal with, divorce, new girlfriend to shack up with…. instead he was sat here. In a white, empty room, wearing the Armani suit he had died in. The room wasn't just white. It was brilliant white, straight out of a scene from Bruce Almighty. He was alone. There was no door, window, person, anything. Why was he here? What now?

Richard thought of Cady. He felt a sudden, sharp pain of something; guilt, loss? Whatever it was, it made his guts ache and his head spin. Is that possible when you're dead? Are you not supposed to be a floating, glowing entity, weightless, naked, at one with the universe? Richard scratched his head and adjusting his tie, got to his feet.

"Hello? Is there anybody there?"

CHAPTER 6

Cady shuffled uncomfortably in her chair. She could feel the multiple mother-of-pearl handled daggers in her back from Cynthia, Richard's auntie and Priscilla. She'd scuttled into the office for the will reading and stuck herself at the back. Richard senior, known as Dick, looked up from his large walnut desk and peered down his reading glasses. He smiled and said, "Cady, honey, come and sit at the front, next to me." Cady felt extremely grateful to him at that moment. He didn't hate her for the funeral debacle! Ignoring the collective tuts and harrumphs from Cynthia and Priscilla, she took her seat and smiled at Dick.

In the room was the four of them, Richard Senior's secretary, a rather dull looking woman dressed entirely in brown suede with angry looking tortoiseshell spectacles, and Marcus, Richard Junior's friend; golf buddy and law associate at the firm. Not many people who meant anything to Richard, Cady noted sadly. Still, at least his parade of strumpets was not here. Yet. She ignored the bucket of ice that careered down her spine and clasped her hands tightly on her lap.

Richard Senior finished reading the papers in front of him and coughed. He shuffled the thick white sheaf of papers and looked at everyone.

"I know that Richard loved you all very dearly and that we have no need for formalities here. Basically, the Will bequeaths something to you all. Cynthia, his art works from office and home are left to you, as he states, his love of the finer things stemmed from you dragging him to the galleries as a child." Cynthia smiled weakly at this, dabbed her weepy eyes with her hanky and reached for Priscilla's hand.

"Priscilla dear, our son left you his baby items, which he states are in a tea chest at his house, and grandfather's gold watch. He said as he had no children, it should return to the family." At the mention

of children, Priscilla crumpled like a soggy paper bag and wept on Cynthia's shoulder. Cady did not know what to do. She knew she should comfort her, but she still felt awkward and ashamed at her unusual behaviour at the funeral, and strangely felt guilty that she had never born a grandchild.
She cleared her throat and spoke. "I am so sorry, Priscilla, I know how much you wanted a grandchild. I am so sorry."
Cady put her head down and wiped at the trickle at her cheek. She too felt robbed at the chance of having a child. 29, no husband, no child, no chance. She felt the familiar anger bubbling up inside her.
Priscilla said nothing, she just kept sobbing with Cynthia shushing her and rubbing her back as one would a toddler.
"Marcus lad, Richard leaves you his golf clubs, and his entire CD collection. He says, and I quote, 'So you can finally improve your handicap and get some decent musical education'."
Marcus grinned and muttered, "Cheeky bugger. I always thrashed him at golf!"
Richard senior smiled, remembering his late son's humour.
"He left me his collection of law books, diplomas and certificates from his law career, to display in my office as a memento. I love that idea. Karen, we shall see to his office this week and get onto that." His secretary Karen nodded reverently and jotted something down on a small notepad.
"Cady, my dear, the rest of his possessions, the house, the car, are all left to you. Richard also had a substantial pension which will divert to you, and some money he had saved. Also some stocks and shares, which I shall be happy to go through with you at a later date, when you are ready dear. And obviously there is a life insurance policy which will pay out to yourself, all debts and the mortgage will be discharged, and the remainder will be reverted to you."
Richard senior and everyone else in the room stared at Cady, nervously awaiting her response. Cady stared at Richard senior, not quite taking it in.
"But Richard, I assumed that the house would come to me as we are joint owners and he was insured, but, the rest…?"
Richard looked at her gently, suddenly understanding. "You may have had your ups and downs with Richard, but you were his wife,

he loved you, he left a letter in the Will detailing everything with a message for you, it's sealed, but shall I read it out n-?"
"No, n-no, please don't." Cady rushed out the words. "It's a bit too much to take in at the moment," she added.
"We understand, Cady, and as for your job here, you can have as much time off as you need, paid of course, we have arranged for a long term temp if you need her, so you just call me when you are ready, okay?"
Cady felt a great rush of affection for her father in law. "Thank you Richard, I…I must be going now, I have a lot to be getting on with."
Richard nodded and handed her a large cream envelope. On the envelope in elegant, swirly letters was her name, in her husband's handwriting. "Everything you need is in there, my dear."
Cady gingerly took the envelope and placed it into her bag.
"Thank you," she muttered heading for the door with her head down. Marcus smiled at her, and opened the door to help her make a quick exit.
Cady walked briskly to the lobby, feeling tired, and strangely nauseous. She raced to the main door, her heels clicking clacking on the polished floor. She could feel people watching her, colleagues, friends, staring at the young widow who lost it at the funeral. She could feel the sweat dripping down her neck; her whole body felt ice cold whilst her cheeks were aflame. She felt so ill. Her ears were ringing and her skin was tingling - what the hell was wrong with her?
She heard her mother-in-law calling her name behind her. Ignoring it, she raced to the doors, burst through into the daylight and lent on the stone pillar outside, enjoying the harsh cold feeling of the brick on her roasting cheek.
"Cady, dear, are you ok, I was just wondering if…"
Cady spun to face Priscilla and her stomach lurched; she vomited down Priscilla's pristine dress, splashing chunks of day-glo orange sick onto her shiny M & S shoes.
Priscilla screamed in surprise, and then throwing her bag to one side to escape the cascade, she stopped and moved closer. Making Cady jump in surprise, he stroked her hands down Cady's back, ssshhing her like her sister had just done to her. "It's ok Cady, let it out, let it all out."

Cady dry retched and stopped when she heard a high pitched keening sound. Oh god, she'd vomited on her mother-in-law and made her cry.
Then she realised that the sound was coming from her and she felt a great release as she sobbed, wailed and cried, her face a mixture of vomit, tears and snot. She finally slowed down and took big teary gasps of breath, her mother-in-law still rubbing her back. The two women stood in shock and silence.
"Cady dear, I do hope that you are ok, Dick and I will always be here for you. I hope you know that. Here dear, a hankie, let's get you cleaned up."
Cady stood sniffing and snuffling loudly. She looked at her mother-in-law; the woman was covered in bright orange vomit, had snot stains on her shoulder pad and smelt like a stale champagne factory. Cady took the hankie and wiped her face. By some miracle the vomit had missed her entirely, save for a splashing on her shoes.
Priscilla looked at her with an expression of sorrow, pity and slight disgust. Her nose was wrinkling at the vomit smell and she was obviously trying her best not to acknowledge it. Georgina would have howled if she was here, Cady thought from nowhere. She would have had it on U-Tube before the sick dried. So many conversations the two had had about the dragon lady that was Cady's mother-in-law, but now, looking at her, she did not feel hatred anymore. She had lost a son after all, had his funeral ruined, and was now staring at a daughter-in-law in tatters. Priscilla would obviously think she was a drink addled lush after the last two meetings. Priscilla's voice suddenly stabbed through her thought pattern, jolting her to the present.
"Cady, are you listening to me dear, you are not well, you need to see a doctor. Are you ok to get home? I…er, obviously can't take you," she said, looking down at her ruined outfit. She pulled a face, pursed her lips and looking back at her daughter-in -law, said, "Darling, is that a Dorito on my Laura Ashley?"

***

Marcus pulled the curtains open and cracked a window in the bay alcove. His eyes brushed over the empty champagne bottles but he

gallantly made no comment. Cady took her shoes off and deposited them into the kitchen bin. No way was that smell ever going to leave those heels. Throwing her bag onto the island worktop, some of the contents scattered out of the opening, the envelope landing closest to her. Cady eyed it suspiciously and slumped onto the nearest breakfast stool. Marcus had got to work in the living room, plumping cushions, taking the bottles and other rubbish out to the recycling bins and straightening things out in his wake. Cady watched him through the open alcove. She had always liked Marcus, he was not as pretentious as the others and even mocked his colleagues. He had been a welcome ally through the many dull Law Society dances, dinner parties and office do's. Being related by marriage to the senior partner and married to the son, Cady's secretary friends had treated her differently, not including her in gossip and bitching as they once did, she was an unknown quantity now in the firm, not quite one of them, but not quite one of the management either. She was never quite accepted in either camp, and this often meant she was out on her own like a pariah. Marcus had obviously noticed this; not that Richard ever did, and his presence had always made things more bearable. Watching him now, tidying up her messy home, she felt a great sense of appreciation that he was there. He had brought her home, never mentioning the vomit or Priscilla, though his eyebrows had gotten tangled in his hairline at the sight of them both outside.
He walked into the kitchen now, patting her shoulder and flicking on the kettle simultaneously. Opening the dishwasher, he took out two clean mugs and started to make tea. Spoon in hand, he suddenly looked thoughtful. "Still two sugars?"
Cady grinned. "Yep. And plenty of milk."
Marcus chuckled. "Sweet tooth as always. So…you feeling better?"
Cady's smile dipped at the memory of Priscilla smothered in puke. "Oh god," she groaned, dropping her head forward onto the cool island surface. "Did I really just do that?"
"Yep," Marcus chortled. "Man, I wish I had seen it happen. That would have been pretty amazing….sorry, but it is funny."
Cady looked up at Marcus, his impish face a mix of sheepish and cheeky. She couldn't stop a little titter erupting, and then a guffaw. Soon, they were both gasping for air, tears rolling down their

cheeks as they laughed hysterically at the vision. Marcus began to laugh like a donkey, slapping the table in hysteria, which sent Cady off into fresh peals of laughter. She laughed till her sides hurt, and then a fresh cascade of tears came, and she was left sobbing again. Marcus stopped laughing and rushed to her side, turning her sideways on the stool to face him and dipping down to her eye level. He threw his arms around her neck and held her close till her crying subsided. Clinging to his shoulders, she released him a little and turned with one hand to reach for a tissue from her bag. Marcus took the tissue from her and stroking her cheeks, he dried her tears. She smiled at him through her tears, grateful that he was there. She was also grateful she had been sucking mints in the car on the way home; her Doritos breath would have probably singed his eyelashes off at these close quarters. His eyelashes were long, so long, and dark, any woman would kill to own a pair like these.
Marcus stopped tending to her face, and cupping her face in his hands, he tentatively moved in and brushed his lips against hers. Pulling away slightly, he licked at his own, tasting her salty tears, and then he slowly moved in again. She took a deep breath and allowed him to kiss her. Cady felt a rush of warmth through her body, and allowed his tongue to part her lips. He tasted of coffee and spearmint, and the scent of him was intoxicating. They explored each others' mouths, slowly and then hungrily, until a loud bang stopped them in their tracks.
Rushing to the window flustered, Cady looked for the cause. Her wedding photo had fallen to the floor, knocked off the side table. It must have been the wind from the open windows. Picking up the picture, she turned to Marcus. The guilt and surprise she felt was mirrored on his face. He looked rattled, as white as a sheet, his hair rumpled, damn..he looked sexy…
"Ah, I had better go, I am so sor.."
"Oh please don't, it's fine, it was me," Cady rushed to silence him. "I..I"
"I had better get back to the office," he said, moving to the door. He turned at the last minute, and forced himself to meet her eye. "You ok?"
Cady was far from it. She was a widow harlot! What had just happened? She knew that if they had not been stopped then she

herself would not have. She would have thrown Marcus onto that island and discovered new territory, marking it with a Cady flag and an intrepid explorer's smile of triumph.

"I'm fine, Marcus, really."

He looked relieved at this, and maybe a flicker of something else? She could not get a read on his expression. Regret? He smiled at her and closed the door behind him, leaving her to the silence in the room, only punctuated by the sound of his retreating car through the open window. Realising she was still holding the picture; she looked down at the two faces encased forever in that happy moment within the silver frame. It had been such a happy day. *I can't deal with this today, she thought.* Opening the side table drawer, she stuffed the photo in face down and slammed it shut, wishing she could stuff her emotions away that easily. Staring at her silent home, she padded upstairs to take a hot shower. And then a cold one for good measure.

CHAPTER 7

Richard jumped to his feet. He moved that frame! He knew it! God, he was so mad! Marcus was supposed to be a mate, what a prick! Richard wished he could take his golf clubs back and insert them into Marcus, one by one. And as for Cady, how could she forget about her husband so easily, so quickly!

"Bastards!" he shouted, pacing up and down the stark white floor. If he hadn't punched that photo frame….but, wait, he hadn't! How could he? He could only watch the scenes that were projected on the white wall before him. He had just concentrated on it, so….he wasn't dead. *That's it*, he thought, *I am not dead. I must be in a coma or something. They buried some sap in my place, maybe 'my' body was unrecognisable. That's it! I am laid in a coma somewhere, and my family think I am dead...so I just need to wake up!*

Genius! How was he going to wake up though? Richard stamped on the spot, so frustrated he felt ready to pop. He grabbed his left arm between his fingers and squeezed, pinching harder and harder at the suited arm. "Wake up, wake up…"Wake up!" he screamed, growling in frustration. "Arrgghhhhh!!! Wake up, damn you, wake up!"

"Honey child, you can't wake up, you're dead."

Richard whirled around at the voice. "Wha…."

In front of him was a large black lady, dressed in a long white dress. The skirt of the dress trailed and swished on the floor beneath her, her black skin a great contrast due to the white brilliance that surrounded them.

"Oh god, what drugs have they got me on?" Richard thought aloud, staring in surprise at the woman walking towards him. "I mean, what a cliché!"

"Cliché am I, honey? Well I am from your imagination precious, so whose fault is that?" She sat on the floor near him and beckoned him to sit. Richard swallowed hard, running his dry tongue over his arid mouth. It felt like rubbing sandpaper on wood. He gingerly edged closer to her, and leaving a sizeable distance between them, flopped down onto his knees.

“I need a drink,” he whispered, “you would think they would keep me hydrated, stuck in a coma. That’s the NHS for you, no private healthcare when you can’t tell them who you are.”
The woman eyed Richard with a slight smile on her face. “Honey, you are dead. Not in a coma, dead. As a doornail. You understand me?”
Richard glared back, “YOU are my imagination! You said that yourself, well buzz off, I don’t want or need you here, I need to get back to my life! Who are you anyway? I don’t know you!”
The woman folded her arms over her more than ample bosoms and exhaled slowly. Looking at him with hooded eyes, she started to speak.
“Richard, honey, I am here to help you with your transition. I look like this because this is how you imagined me. You got hit by a car, and you died. You are not in a coma, you are in transition. Or the unfinished business department, as we call it up here.” She chuckled at her own joke, her hefty cleavage bobbing up and down.
“Bollocks,” spat Richard. “What’s this place then, Heaven?” he scoffed.
“No honey, that’s next, when you are ready.”
Her words sent a chill down his spine. “Ready? Ready? I am not fucking ready!! I am 34! If I am to play along with this little hallucination, then tell me, how come I can see my family down there? How come I am not a floaty ghost? And how come I just tossed that photo frame around? Huh, you got an answer for that lady?”
The rotund woman pulled herself to her feet, and straightening out her dress, she smiled at him. Which just infuriated him further.
“Come on then, HOW?”
“First of all, she replied, wagging her chubby polished index finger at him, “you do not speak to me like that boy; vision or no vision, I have feelings. You can call me Gerty. No cussing, and no hissy fits. You is a grown man, and will damn well act like one in my company, d’you here?”
Richard’s eyes nearly popped out. This woman had attitude. Better not annoy her further. “Yes, Gerty.”
“Good,” Gerty nodded. “Now, as for the photo frame, the newly crossed, that’s you, they have some residual energy left from their

lives. If people die suddenly, before their time then that energy buzzes around their spirit with nowhere to go. You channelled that energy because your emotional state spiked. Basically, you got ticked off, honey, and your spirit punched that frame. It will cross over with you when you go, the anger can't. That's why you are here, your spirit is not ready to let go."
Richard had been shaking his head vigorously throughout. It couldn't be true, it just couldn't. He surveyed the strange woman in front of him. He was in a bad Martin Laurence movie, on repeat. He had to wake up.
"Richard honey, you are dead. Don't think I can't hear those thoughts of yours, whirling round that big fat old head of yours. I will prove it, you want a drink, think of one."
"What?"
"THINK of a drink, go on."
Richard puffed his cheeks out. Oh well, better humour her. At least this way he can prove he was right and get rid of her. Closing his eyes, he visualised a drink. His dry mouth watered at the mere thought of refreshment.
"Open your eyes, honey."
Richard peeked out from behind one lid. He slumped forward, head in his hands. At his crossed feet stood a bottle of Evian, and a glass of ice, as though plucked right from his own head.

CHAPTER 8

Cady awoke to the sound of pounding. "Muurr?" she slurred, lifting her head from the pillow. She was in the spare room, legs and arms akimbo on the double sofa bed. Sitting up quickly, she gipped as a wave of nausea overpowered her. Oh Lord, she felt ill. "When did I last eat anything?" she asked herself aloud. Stumbling out of the guest room, she zombie walked to the bathroom. Not a pretty sight, she thought, horrified as a baggy-eyed wild-haired bush woman stared back at her from behind the mirror. Impending birthday, yeah right! Cady looked like she was hurtling towards a half century, not flirty 30! She scraped her blonde straggles back into a ponytail using the ever present bobble from her wrist, when she heard pounding again. Oh yeah…what was that?
Walking into the front master bedroom she peered out from behind the curtains. The sight behind those drapes made her want to curl up into a microscopic ball and float away on one of the many dust motes fluttering around the light. Bugger! Priscilla and Cynthia, looking like two floral specials from the elderly sofa catalogue, were peering through the downstairs windows, taking it in turns to tut, mutter to each other and pound on the front door. Oh my god, what are THEY doing here! She had a phone! Cady then realised that she had pulled the landline socket out of the wall last night, and she hadn't switched her mobile on since…..well, just since. Georgie! Shit! Cady palm slapped her own forehead. Georgina was going to kill her, and she was due back from Paris today. Double bugger.
She could not deal with this today, no chance. Peering down again to see if they had gone, Cady looked straight into the upturned podgy faces of the dumpy duo. Damn, busted. Cady sagged, waved wanly and headed downstairs to open the door.

***

An hour later, Cady was wrapped up on the sofa, tea and bacon sandwich in hand, swaddled in patchwork blankets (obviously brought from home, Richard would never have allowed such a thing to cross the front door) staring at the Kim and Aggy monstrosity that was currently tearing through her nooks and crannies.

As they worked, primping, scrubbing, dusting and bleaching everything in sight, they took it in turns to keep silence at bay, chattering away at Cady, and not waiting for a reply.
"Have your parents been in touch at all, Cady dear?"
"I am not sure to be honest Priscilla; I don't actually know where my phone is at present. (It was stuffed under the spare bed, along with the letter from Richard). I never knew my dad. I saw mum before the funeral, but not since. We are not that close."
"Hum," Priscilla bristled, pursing her lips. She obviously had an opinion but chose to keep it to herself. Cady appreciated that. Hugging her hot mug to her, she sipped at the tea, wishing the nausea would pass. The bacon sandwich smelt delicious, her mouth was watering, but the thought of eating it left her cold. Priscilla seemed to notice her lack of eating. "Cady, dear, you need to eat." She bent to pick up a stack of law magazines from under the coffee table. Seeing what she had in her hands, she wilted, sinking into the armchair.
"You can take those Priscilla, give them to Dick."

Priscilla smiled up at her. "Thank you darling. And actually honey, Cyn and I came to see if we could pick up the things that Richard left to us, if that's not too premature? We would just dearly love to be close to his things, if that makes sense."
Cady nodded slowly. Personally, she could not bear to see his things, let alone be near them, but she kept that thought to herself.
"Erm, sure, sure….the tea chest is in his study and the art is…around." She gestured about the room vaguely, almost spilling her hot drink as she did so. She slumped again, clinging to the cup like a ship wreck survivor would to a lifebelt. Priscilla and Cynthia exchanged worried looks and then headed upstairs to get the things and tidy up.

Walking into the master bedroom, Priscilla exhaled sharply as she saw the king size bed, a picture of Cady smiling out from a silver frame on one dresser, next to a Steve Jobs autobiography. This must have been Richard's side, she thought sadly. Cady's side had been made, but Richard's was left tousled. She could still make out the head imprint on the pillow. The urge to draw that pillow to her

and breathe in the scent of her son overpowered her, and she clasped her hands behind her back to stop herself. She got a flashback of Richard as a curly haired toddler, all dimples and chocolate covered cheeks. She must have sniffed that boy's neck ten times a day from birth till the day he made her stop. *"Mum, I'm 15! For heaven's sake, stop sniffing me!"*
She smiled at the memory; if she could have bottled that scent she would have inhaled it every day since. Cynthia jolted her from her daydream by entering the room.
"She has not slept in here since, has she? You can tell."
Priscilla nodded. "Poor child, she does not know what to do, does she? Do you think it's true, Cilla, was he seeing someone else?"

Priscilla looked at the photo on the dresser and then around the room. It was so masculine, all browns and blues and nothing feminine at all, no dresser, trinkets, just a few books and expensive fitted wardrobes. The only hint that a woman ever lived here was that picture. She sniffed and looked at Cynthia kindly.
"He was his father's son, Cyn, I will bet my Chanel he was."

The two women left another hour later, Priscilla's driver stuffing their Range Rover Vogue to the grilles with Richard's possessions. Cady felt utterly shattered, drained of whatever energy she had. Time to reattach to the outside world, she supposed. Plugging the land line back into the wall, it rang instantly, making her jump. Heart racing, she lifted the receiver to her ear. "Cady? Cady? Is that you?"
Shit. Georgie sounded mad. "Hi, George, yeah it's me. You back?"
"Back? Am I back? I have been back since last night. Where the fuck have you been? Both your phones were out, I knocked last night and got no answer, all the lights were off, Jesus! I am so pissed off with you! Are you ok?"
Cady suddenly laughed at her irate friend. "Sorry, sorry, I know, I have been a bit out of it, and I never heard you last night, I went to bed early. Sorry hun. You coming over? I could actually use your help."
"Come round? You really are a cheeky cow, Cady, wanting a favour after I have been running round like a blue arsed fly."

Silence hummed down the line. Cady grimaced. She had been a bit bad to let her friend worry, she had been great through all this. Maybe asking a favour was a bit cheeky.
"So, I have white or red here. Chinese, curry? I will be there in 30 minutes. Get the glasses out, plates warmed and arse in gear. Ok?"
Cady smiled into the phone. She loved her friend to bits.
"Ok, arse gear engaging now."
"Good, and take a shower, cos I bet you look like a bag lady and I am not staring at that sight all night," Georgina chuckled, "and find your mobile. We will deal with any messages together, understand?"
"Deal." Cady replaced the receiver and sniffed a pit. Yeuch, George had a point. She stripped off, threw her clothes straight into the washer, and headed upstairs, leaving the door on the latch. No chance on the phone though, she would just pretend to have lost it. That was a job for another day.

***

Cady giggled as Neve Campbell ran from Ghostface, straight up the stairs, past the exit. "Seriously, why don't they just run out of the front door, first thing I would do!"
"I know!" George agreed, stuffing another prawn cracker into her mouth. They were both sat cross legged on the sofa, a Chinese buffet surrounding them, a bottle of pinot grigio open on the coffee table. "These slasher flicks give us chicks a bad rep, casting us as big boobed bimbos who faint at the first sight of a bit of blood..I mean, sheesh!"
Cady suddenly got a clear image of blood in her mind. From that night, on the pavement…so much blood, and the noise……she gulped and reached for her glass, draining the contents. She noticed Georgie studying her, prawn cracker hanging from her bottom lip. "I'm fine George, don't worry."
Georgina covered her best friend's hand with her own. Cady attempted to grin at her, but it showed on her face as a pained, twisted grimace.
"You want to talk about it Cade? You never did say what happened…"
"NO! Er..no, I don't."
George left it there. She knew not to push her friend. They had been mates that many years that they each knew what the other

was going to do before they moved a muscle, she knew that Cady would talk when she felt ready. IF she ever felt ready.
"Right well, obviously slasher flicks were a humongous fuck up faux-pas on my part, how about a bit of Edward Cullen?" She waved the DVD of Breaking Dawn at her.
"Sure that sounds great. But remember, I am and ALWAYS will be Team Jacob, you can keep your boring vamp, give me a hot blooded wolf any day."
Cady continued to fork more chicken and cashew nuts and fried rice into her mouth. Man she was starving tonight! She had already polished off the prawn toast, and even as she was eating she couldn't stop her mind wandering to the large tub of Phish Food that was in the freezer. Mind you, she had not eaten much, it wouldn't do her any harm to binge tonight.
"I have my appointment at the clap clinic tomorrow. I am dreading it. Thought my days of worrying about STDs were over, being married and all."
"Hmmm," replied Georgina. Cady glanced at her friend. She was sat beside her on the couch, slim legs encased in skinny designer jeans, Pandora bracelet clinking against her wine glass. Her tight white top showed off her toffee tan, and her nails as always were buffed, polished and perfect.
"Are you not listening to me?"
"Huh?" George jumped at her voice. "Oh, sorry mate, I am listening, really I am. I just have a few things on my mind at the minute, nothing to worry about."
Reaching for the DVD remote, she paused Bella mid-gurn. Why did that girl never smile, with two hot guys after her?
"Spill it. Now."
George ran her hand through her hair, and avoiding Cady's gaze, took a large gulp of wine.
"Cady, I love you, you know that, but I am worried about you. You are acting like you have been dumped, not…not.."
"Widowed?" Cady offered, raising her eyebrows. "I WAS dumped George, he left me for another woman and then he died. End of. If he had been alive he would have still been gone. With HER." She spat that last word out with venom and went to take her now empty plate to the dishwasher. George followed, glass in hand.

"I know Cady, but he died! Your husband died! You are not grieving; I haven't seen you cry…"
"I HAVE CRIED!" She shouted back, slamming the plate into the dishwasher in anger. "I have!" Cady remembered the last time she had cried over Richard, when she fell into Marcus's arms and then…. Her cheeks flushed as she thought of Marcus's lips, the way his hair felt between her fingers. She shook her head at the memory and turned to face George.
"George, I have cried, ok? I can't grieve for him because it feels fake. He left me! What am I, a divorcee, a widow? I just don't know how to feel, I just hate him SO MUCH, I can't help it."
George made a move towards her, stopping when Cady motioned to stop her.
"No Cady, you don't hate him, you are grieving. You have to, you are making yourself ill, shutting yourself away like this, and you look awful. I bet that meal is the first proper thing you have eaten in days, and what the hell happened in here?"
George motioned to the blank spaces on the walls and the sparse look of the room. Following her worried expression, Cady had to take note of what her friend was seeing. She had pretty much given everything of Richard's away from downstairs. Upstairs was a different story, she had shown the driver where the tea chest was and then locked the study door behind him. She could not deal with seeing his office, or his things in their room yet, and she didn't want the two biddies loose up there either.
Fortunately, they had both took a look at Cady and ordered her right to bed, then bustled away with their booty.
"Richard's mother and aunt came, they were left some things in the will, ok? I don't want to look at his stuff." Cady sat down at the breakfast bar, her mouth small and weak now. "Look mate, I am fine, alright? I wanted to ask you tonight if you would help me with Richard's things from upstairs, but I see now that you are not the best person to ask. I don't want to fall out. Please. I really just don't have the energy this evening."
George nodded. "Ok, well I have to go. Please Cady, leave his stuff. Just for a little while. You might regret it later and then it will be too late."
George kissed her pale cheek, put on her cream wool coat and left.

Cady sat on the stool, utterly shattered and deplete of everything and anything. She looked around the bare open plan living area. This place had never felt like home, she had never felt like it was hers. Richard chose everything from the carpets to the curtains to the type of washing powder they used. When had she become this meek follower? No-one knew the truth, not really. Cady had felt disjointed for years, not quite alive. Richard was a fine husband, he worked hard, showed her affection and care, remembered their anniversary. Stuff of perfection, right? Everyone seemed to think so, everywhere they went people admired them, wanted to be them, this happy, rich loved up couple. They did not know the truth though. She did not love Richard, hadn't for a while. Because this wasn't the first time he had cheated on her. And tomorrow would not be the first time she had been humiliated at the sexual health clinic either.

CHAPTER 9

Waking up in her luxurious apartment, Georgina Elliott heard the click of the coffee maker. Ah, Magda was here. George slipped out of her Egyptian cotton sheets, pulled her silk kimono over her black lace negligee, and let her nose take her to the kitchen. Turning her thoughts to the previous night, she remembered how ill and frail Cady looked. She had to speak to someone, get her some help. Her parents would do more harm than good, best they are not worried with this, and Richard's family had lost a son themselves. Apart from each other, they only had work colleagues, they had never felt the need for a large circle of friends. Her aunt, she suddenly thought. Of course! She had brought her up after all, she would get through to Cady, and she would know how to help. Feeling better already, she resolved to ring her first thing. Together they would come up with a plan to help her. Georgina brightened at the thought of helping her friend. She just hated to see her like this. Richard had a bloody lot to answer for, that was for sure. If it hadn't been a taxi that had hit him, she might have thought it was some wronged woman trying to take him out for the sake of humanity and the safety of women everywhere. They could probably plead insanity under the Scourge of the Sleazeball act too. Entering the kitchen, she was suddenly starving.

Her small, broad maid, Magda, was emptying the dishwasher and laying out croissants and Danish pastries. "Good morning, Miss Elliott, you sleep well, yes?"
George slid into a seat at the small round table, smiling at the sound of her name in Hungarian born Magda's broken English accent.
"I keep telling you Maggie, it's Georgina, ok?"
"Oh yes miss, I mean Georgina," Magda stuttered, turning to put some cream in a bowl. Pouring out a fresh coffee into George's favourite mug, adorned with Eric Northman, True Blood's Viking vamp, she set the steaming hot coffee in front of her.
"Magda, get a coffee, come sit with me, I will never eat all this."

Magda did as she was asked, and taking a sip of her own, visibly relaxed.
"Seriously girl, you have been working for me now for almost six months, chill out, ok?" George giggled and patted the maid's slender arm.
Magda smiled back at her. "Ok. Is deal."
The sound of the phone startled them both. The machine kicked in, and George's honeyed tones filled the silence. At the beep, a man's voice, deep and husky, echoed around the room. "Ah, yes, er, hello. I got your number from the agency, my name is Ben Morton, and I would like to discuss using your services."
George grinned sheepishly at Magda, and picking up the cordless, walked to the bedroom, closing the door behind her. Magda shrugged and bit into an apricot Danish.
Shrugging, she wolfed down the rest of the stodgy pastry and sat back to finish her coffee. English folk are so strange, she mused.

CHAPTER 10

Cady ran up the clinic steps, heels sploshing beneath her, brolly unfurled above. Standing on the large stone steps, she leant against a pillar and struggled to close it down. For all the good it had done anyway; she was soaked to the skin. Having opted for a smart black skirt suit that morning, her black suede heels were now utterly destroyed and the water squidged beneath her toes as she moved. Her blouse had gone transparent under her black jacket, showing off her white and pink lace bra. Great, now she looked like a street walker picking up free condoms. Her thick red wool coat covered her skirt, but was open at the bust, which only made the effect worse.

She struggled to close the umbrella, ignoring the looks from gawping, equally wet passersby. "Oh feck it!" She finally exclaimed, dragging wet tendrils of hair out of her eyes. Stabbing the umbrella into the nearest bush viciously, she sloshed her way through the double doors.

The clinic was based in a converted old building, all high white ceilings and mosaic tiling. The lobby was huge and quite bare, aside from a two seater couch which was opposite from a glass partitioned reception desk. A door next to the couch had a laminated sign blu-tacked to it, with WAITING ROOM in big black letters. *God, I hope no-one I know is behind those doors.* Then again, didn't everyone feel that way in a place like this? Even though family planning does a range of services, tell someone you are 'off to the clinic' and everyone suddenly gets a visual of tiny crustaceans crawling round your gusset, right? Time to get this over with.

She straightened herself out and tried to assemble her long hair into some sort of a style. Slinging her oversized handbag at her feet, narrowly missing the small puddle of water that was emanating from her feet, she tapped on the glass partition. The panel slid across and a petite, perky blonde receptionist beamed at her.

"Hello, can I help you?"

Cady squinted against the mega-watt bright smile and returned a slightly dimmer one of her own, licking her lip discreetly as a large droplet of rainwater landed on it from her soaked hair.
"Hi, I have an appointment, Cady.."
"First names are fine dear, we pride ourselves on being discreet here. Take a seat my darling." Another earth shatteringly wide smile showed off two tight rows of perfect teeth. Cady gurned back at her and walked into the waiting room. It was empty. Thank the Lord. Shaking off her sodden coat, she draped it on the back of a plastic chair nearest the radiator and sat down. Checking her bag, she was relieved that the contents were untouched by the torrential downpour outside. She was glad that Georgina was coming round again with food and a DVD.
Cady smiled at the thought of her friend. Man she had a good job. It might be IT and boring computers all day, but the jetting around was pretty cool. Furthest she had ever been was Lanzarote when she was first with Richard. After that work took off and he never had the time, although he did manage a fair few golfing weekends with the firm. Wives and girlfriends were always invited too, to take up residence in the bar and spa all weekend. Weekends of pure hell, living on wheatgrass juice shoots, being plucked and pummelled like a chicken carcass, and all the time having to listen to 'the ladies that lunch' drone on about insolent nannies, incompetent maids and the service at Marks and Spencer's Food Halls. They lived in a different world, and Cady never wished to travel to that realm. They were like Stepford Wives, and we all know how that ends. No thank you, she thought.
Looking around the white and green painted waiting room, she marvelled at the leaflets on the rack nearby. Scary things jumped out at her, words like genital warts, female condom, and diaphragm. Oh dear God. On the wall next to her was a poster showing a pink penis and balls with a spotty 'face' and sad expression. The caption next to it read 'Will's spots really hampered his social life.' Cady laughed out loud before she remembered where she was.
"Cady?"
She jumped at the sound of the voice. A smartly dressed woman in a grey trouser suit had appeared from a door that Cady had not even noticed before.

“Er, yes, sorry.” Cady collected her bag and followed the woman through the door.
“I’m Trudy,” she said as she entered a door marked ‘treatment.’
“Take a seat,” she said, smiling and pointing to a red plastic chair.
Cady sat in the chair, suddenly nervous.
“So, how can I help you today?” Trudy was obviously one of these jolly women; you could tell she would be a laugh after a couple of Babychams. Cady cleared her throat.
“Er…hum…he hur..I need a sexual health check; you see my husband has been unfaithful.” *Again, she added silently.*
Trudy smiled sympathetically, her green eyes crinkling at the corners.
“Right, well first of all we need to do a urine sample.”
“I…er, brought one.” *I had a spare piss pot from last time, she added to herself.*
“Ah, great stuff,” Trudy replied, snapping on a pair of latex gloves from a box on her desk. “Is it fresh from this morning?”
“Yes,” Cady replied.
“Brilliant.” Trudy took the sample from Cady and taking it out of the La Senza carrier bag (another tell tale sign that she was a lady of the night, Cady grimaced) she dipped a stick into it, leaving it on a napkin on the mahogany surface of the desk.
“So my dear, have you had any symptoms at all?”
Cady shuffled in her seat, the hard plastic making her bottom ache. Her clothes were still very wet too, which made her feel even more wretched. She concentrated on one of the thick green striped curtains while she considered her own health. She had been in a bit of a blur recently.
“Do you have any symptoms?”
“Well, I have noticed I need the toilet more often, and I am a bit tired, but other than that, no, I don’t think so.”

Trudy nodded and made notes in her file. Her writing was long and loopy, Cady couldn’t make out the words from where she was sitting.
“And contraception?” She asked, ticking some boxes on a chart.
“Ah, no, well I was on the pill, but I stopped taking it.” *Didn’t seem to be any point, they weren’t having sex anymore anyway.*

"And did you have unprotected sex with your husband after this time?"
Cady brushed back her now damp and frizzy hair. In the humidity of this room, she estimated looking like Worzel Gummidge within the hour. She thought back over the last few months, there was only the one night, the Law Society dinner, 4 months ago.
It had been a good night, actually, best for a while. Cady brought her attention back into the room and looked at Trudy. Trudy was not looking at her; she was bringing the stick out of the pot and staring at it closely. If she got any closer she could touch it actually. Oh God, Cady thought. He's done it to me again! Richard, you utter bastard, she shouted in her own head, you have done it again, and what was it this time? Parasites, syphilis, leprosy of the hoo-ha? She felt the lurch of her stomach and her heart pumped widely. She heard a sudden ringing in her ears, and everything distorted into a tunnel like shape.
"Er, only once, at Christmas," she replied weakly. Her voice sounded strange in her own ears. She stood up, her hands shaking. Jesus, she was going to…to…and then everything went black and Cady hit the deck.

CHAPTER 11

Luke sat hunched over his desk, poring over plans for a 5 bed extension in Morley. His dad was a bugger for detail, and Luke wanted to leave nothing to chance. He already ribbed him constantly about 'wasting' his talent. Having studied Civil and Architectural Engineering at The University of Bath, with a prestigious placement at the Royal Academy of Arts in London, his parents had fully expected him to land a top job designing skyscrapers in America, or creating housing projects in Dubai. When he actually moved into an apartment and declared that he was destined to be an artist, or as his dad called it, 'a penniless bum' their enthusiasm had waned somewhat. Well, not Mum of course, she agreed with her husband and made all the right noises in public but told Luke regularly that as long as he followed his creative streak, and his heart, and was happy in life, than so was she. 'After all,' she would say, with a cheeky glint in her eye, 'if you are not poor and tortured, then you are not a true creative spirit.' Luke always remembered that, and even though rent was tough some months, and he couldn't afford a car, he was thrilled with his life, and with Dad coming round to the idea and offering him more and more freelance work, things were getting easier. And as he always retorted to his dad when he snuck a sly dig in at his son's expense, if he ever needed the money, truly needed it, he had kept his hand in, had an excellent education and could land a highly paid job pretty much anywhere. Till then, he loved his thrifty life, his apartment full of canvases and brushes, and his beans on toast diet.

He did pay into a good pension however, his dad had insisted on that, and having no debts, he figured he would be okay for a few years yet.

Checking and rechecking the plans again, he was pleased with his work. This project was going to be fun, he was almost sad to hand it over to the building team. The couple had asked for a post-modern, contemporary art deco feel, and his dad had visibly paled at the idea, and passed the plan making and finer details onto Luke with a grunting respect to his knowledge in the area. He could tell his dad had no idea what the thin couple dressed in scarves and

ironic t-shirts were on about. It was a bit of a mish-mash of ideas, but Luke had made it work, they had agreed the initial plans, paid a deposit and set a date. It was to be their biggest project in years, Dad having slowed his company down a lot in his twilight years, paring down his once large company to a handful of trusted workers, and a couple of vans. He had given up his large commercial offices and now ran the business from his custom built home office, jutting off from the main house, all built from scratch of course. His mum had a studio at the bottom of the garden for her writing and painting and she was always locked away on some project or another, only emerging during daylight hours to feed her 'boys' which included all the workers, to tend the garden, or to read novels in the sun lounger, drinking wine, whatever the weather. It was fair to say his mother was unique. Luke smiled to himself at the thought, and hearing the coffee machine click off, he turned with his half empty mug of cold coffee to get a refill and jazz the brain up. He turned with the mug and....rammed it straight into a pair of tiny bosoms, promptly dumping coffee straight down the barely there cleavage.
"Aaahh!" Victoria screeched, shivering as the cold drops of Columbian blend spread into an ugly stain on her white cashmere v-neck.
"Oh shit, sorry I-" Luke stopped and stared, catching flies at the sight of his ex before him. "What the hell are you doing here?"

"Oh, Luke, that's not nice now is it. Jesus Christ, my top is ruined. Still as clumsy as ever I see," Victoria scowled, grabbing a tissue from the desk to futilely dab at the brown stain. Tutting loudly, she scowled at him. "Well. It's jolly well ruined now, isn't it. Thanks a bunch." Crossing her arms at her sides, she whipped off the ruined top, flicking her platinum blonde hair back off her face in the same movement. Luke recognised the pendant round her neck. Now standing there in her white (also coffee stained) bra and tight black trousers, she noticed his flash of recognition at the object. Playfully, she smoothed down her bra using both hands to rub over her breasts. Luke flushed and looked away quickly. Damn, she still knew how to play him. It had been a while though. Luke felt a stirring in his pants and his face flushed further. *Damn you penis! Show some taste. This woman is poison. Down, boy, down.*

"I repeat my question. What the hell are you doing here?"
Victoria had the good sense to look ashamed.
"I know we didn't have the best parting Lukie, but I am sorry…but as you can see," she stroked the pendant, a pure black heart on a matching black string, "I have always kept you close to me." At the last words, she moved her hand to her mouth, biting her index finger coquettishly. Luke shuddered inwardly. *How did he ever fall for this woman?*
Straightening up, Luke went to swill his cup out and filled it with strong black coffee. Not even bothering to add his usual bucket of milk and one sugar, he swigged at the treacle-like substance, enjoying the jolt from the caffeine hit.
"Funny isn't it, Vic, how I made the heart black? It was almost as if I knew you were a cold hearted bitch from the beginning. Now if you don't mind, I have work to do, so if you could take your breasts and yourself out of my office, I would be extremely grateful." He strode to his desk and sat down with his back to her, swigging his drink.
Victoria opened her mouth to say something, but then her shoulders sagged, and picking up her top, she walked to the door.
"Oh, and Vic?" Luke said, his back still turned to her.
Victoria swung around, hopeful. "Yes, Luke?"
He swung around in his office chair, smiling broadly. She brightened, returning his smile.
"Don't forget to send me the dry cleaning bill, will you."
Luke smirked and turned around again. Ok, it was a cheap shot, and he hated to be nasty, it just wasn't in his nature, but man this girl pushed his buttons.
Victoria half growled/screamed. "Gggrraarrgghh! Oh Luke, you really are a stubborn pig!" and she stampeded toward the door. Pulling it angrily, she came face to face, or rather breasts to face, with Luke's dad.
"Ah, Victoria, found it ok did we?"
His eyes crinkled with amusement at the scene. Victoria, in her bra, looking angry, embarrassed and shocked all at the same time. Luke was staring at his father wild-eyed.
"What do you mean Dad, 'found it ok'? You *asked* her to come?"
"Yes son, I did," his dad replied, pouring himself a coffee. "We need some help around here, we will be busy on this project, and I

don't want to be turning work down, that's just silly, so Victoria here will be joining the team full time. After all, we have the first in the class working here, so why not the second?"

Victoria folded her arms and shot Luke a smug 'you are stuck with me' look. Luke was horrified. Oh God Dad, you have to be kidding me, he thought.
The atmosphere was still begging for a knife to cut it when his dad piped up.
"First rule of business though, Vic dear, we do wear full office gear here. Apart from naked Fridays of course!" He laughed at his own witty remark.
Victoria flushed and covered her modesty with her ruined sweater. Luke covered his head with his hands and slammed his forehead onto his desk.

CHAPTER 12

"Hello, Cady, can you hear me?"
Cady's cheek was freezing. She could feel the cold running icy fingers through her body, replacing the previous hot, clammy feeling with an even worse chilly, goose bump feeling. She shivered.
"Cady, Cady dear, are you ok?" There was that voice again, she thought. What do you want, little voice? Leave me alone, eh, jog on and bother someone else. It might be a bit cold here, but it was quite nice. I could just stay here, be quite happy, peaceful. Trudy. Oh yes, the voice was Trudy. Then it all came screaming back. She was in the clinic. She must have passed out. Oh Christ, she did, she passed out! And she had a disease. The woman had been just about to tell her. Trenchfoot of the vagina. Galloping piaka of the flaps. Oh..no. She thought of last time, the itch, the burning when she peed. The knowing look on the nurse's face when she had a peek down south. She silently cursed Richard. I hope his dick rots off, she said in her own head. Oh..of course, it would now..he was dead. She moaned slightly. Things were so messed up.
"Get me a glass of water please, Ange, I think she's coming round," Trudy said. Cady peeked out from behind one eyelid. Trudy smiled at her, another woman with red curly hair and a glass of water in her long gold painted talons by her side. Angie smiled at her, placed the water on the desk and left discreetly.
Cady sat up slowly. "I am so sorry," she said, making an attempt to sort out her hair before she remembered it was a frizz bombed rain soaked birds nest. She chuckled at the hilarity of it all, and then she started to cry. Trudy patted her arm, and this was her undoing. She erupted into choking retching sobs, and it all spilled out, Richard's affairs, her devastation, his leaving her. She did not tell her about his death, about the accident, she just couldn't think about that yet, let alone put it into words to tell someone else. She cried and cried, until she was a snuffling wreck on the chilly tiled floor. Trudy was nodding and rubbing her back with her hand, just as Priscilla did. *Why did people do this?* Cady wondered in passing. It was nice though, oddly soothing and mumsy.

Trudy passed her a tissue. "Feeling better now, hun?" she said kindly.
"Cady smiled and blew her nose. "Yes I do thanks," she got up and they both sat back in their chairs. "You can tell me Trudy, what do I have?"
Trudy looked nonplussed for a second. "Have?"
Cady frowned, wiping ineffectually with a clean tissue at her panda eyes. "Er, yes, you said that something showed up?"
"Ah," Trudy said, pursing her lips. "Well, in light of the situation, with what you just told me…can I call someone to be here with you, pick you up?"
Cady twigged. "Oh God! I have Aids, haven't I! That's why you want someone here! It's bad, isn't it!" Cady fought against the pinprick of tears forming in her eyes and looked pleadingly at Trudy. "Just tell me, please."
Trudy shook her head vigorously. "It's not Aids, we can't tell that from a urine sample, you would need a blood test. But there is something." Biting her lip, she paused. "Cady, you're pregnant. And, I suspect anaemic but your GP and midwife will sort that out sharpish."
Cady gawped at her, sucking air like a fish out of water. *"I'm what!?"*
Marcus picked up his office phone and dialled out; slamming it back down before it connected. Massaging his temple with his broad fingers he banged his fist on his desk. Damn it, he couldn't get that kiss out of his head. It was driving him crazy, he wanted to be with her, helping her, supporting her but he knew that now it would be confusing and might make Cady feel worse about her new situation as a widow. He loved Richard dearly, they had been mates for years, right from being fresh faced hopefuls studying and partying together through university and Marcus had been chuffed to bits when Richard had told him his dad was looking for a solicitor within his firm. It had all worked out so well, till he met Cady. And *he* did meet Cady first. In the Barristers bar, knocking back pints one Friday night after a particularly ball busting week at work, and this girl had walked in with her mates. She was beautiful. Marcus clocked her straightaway and sat watching mesmerised. This girl was something else, she came in giggling with her mates in a figure hugging cream shift dress, simple heels

and an amazing smile. She was up for a laugh too, giggling away with her mates, egging them on to order shots. Marcus drained his pint and stood up to make his introductions, when Richard came out of the toilet, strode to the bar and pretty much just asked her straight out. He was all charms as usual, Richard could be funny back then, and he cracked jokes and soon won her girl friends over, and that was that. Marcus was left in the sidelines while they chatted away, seemingly oblivious to their respective entourages. It turned out she worked for Abbott and Mansell, a rival firm and her legal secretary mates proceeded to cop off, one by one, with the ridiculously grateful and normally reserved solicitors from *his* firm. When Richard eventually kissed Cady, much later, on the nightclub dancefloor while their work mates cavorted together around them, Marcus gave up all hope of making his move and proceeded to get extremely pissed instead. So now here they were, her a widow, and him as in love with her as ever. Bad timing was the understatement that poked in his mind continually. When *would* their time be though? Would there *be* a time now? Considering the option of having Cady as a friend or nothing at all, Marcus would always choose friend. If he could get more eventually, then all the better, but not having her at all made his stomach turn. Picking up the phone, he dialled the number and twirling the cord around his fingers till his skin went white, he held his breath. It rang out, out, out. Damn, machine picked up. Exhaling quickly, he left a message. "Hi Cady, it's me, er Marcus. Listen, I just wanted to check if you were ok so please, call me ok? Thanks, and it's Marcus, call me. Thanks. Hope you are ok. Bye bye," The machine cut him off, signalling the end of his rambling. Marcus put down the phone and cringed. Smooth move, Marcus, he chided himself. What a douche. He threw his pen at the office door in frustration, only for it to open and the biro to hit Angela in the face.
"Ouch! Marcus!"
"Shit, sorry!" Marcus jumped to his feet, forcing his swivel chair back against his bookcase. Angela rubbed her nose and scooped to pick the pen up.
"Bad day?"
Marcus looked sheepish and smoothed his rumpled clothes down. "Er, something like that, bad month I think."

"Oh, not all bad I hope," she said playfully. "Lunch?"
Marcus looked at Angela and tried in vain to think of a reason. God she was nice looking, she looked fit to eat in her ivory silk blouse and tight charcoal pencil shirt. And those fuck me heels, well, they had already gotten him into trouble. He cringed again, this time at the memory of the night of the funeral. A drunken flirtation and a bottle of JD resulting in a frenzied shag on his living room rug. Since then, he had been avoiding Angela like one would a leper or a swamp monster, avoiding calls, being alone with her; she was getting more and more determined though. Eventually they would have to have 'the talk,' he was sure of it but for now he would rather swerve that little chat. Angela was a very hard as steel solicitor type, all balls and no baking, as they would say, and she was not a woman to be crossed by any means. The fact is, he didn't even like her personality; sure the package was smoking hot but he could never have a relationship with her, even if he wasn't already hung up on Cady. Truth was, that night he was drunk, sad and lonely and after seeing Cady's outburst and sudden departure, he had slipped into a dark mood and Angela had just simply been there.
Aware that she was now staring at him questioningly and tapping her slender foot, he cleared his throat quickly and started to shuffle papers on his desks. "Er no, sorry, I can't, too much on, been playing catch up since Richard..you know, picked up his cases too while they find a replac…a new solicitor."
Angela clenched her jaw and tossed her head, flicking her hair away from her face. "Yes well, Richard left a large hole in..the firm. I will leave you to it."

Marcus smiled in relief at her retreating back and jumped when she twirled around to face him. "BUT, Marcus dear, we DO have to talk. Friday night, La Rustico, 8pm. No raincheck, ok?"
Her stern set face showed she would book no refusal. Marcus tried to smile at her, only managing to bear his gums in a wolf-like grimace, and nodded. "See you then," he said through suddenly dry lips, his whole mouth making a smacking sound at the words. Angela beamed back and power walked back to her office, barking orders to book a table at her brow-beaten secretary on the way

past. Marcus went to sit in his chair, instead hitting the floor and laying there with his legs in the air.
Bollocks, he thought, rubbing his elbow, which had hit the desk on the way down. Friday. Great, he now had less than 4 days to either contract the zombie virus, flee the country or face the music.
Eating brains looked good about now.

CHAPTER 13

Cady walked out of the clinic with Trudy running after her. "Er, Cady, I don't think you should be alone right now, please wait till I call someone, ok? Please?"
Cady rounded on her. "Thank you for your concern, but I am fine. I will make an appointment with my GP for a blood test like you said, but for now I just want to be alone."
She stormed down the path, heels smashing into the pebbled driveway. She was, was…furious! Pregnant! Jesus Christ! What the hell was she going to do now??? Pregnant and widowed by 30 was not the life plan of anyone, any careers advisor at school would surely baulk at that one. *Well, Miss, when I grow up, I want to marry a total bastard, get knocked up, then be a single parent no man in his right mind will touch!* Cady was walking fast now, through the town, past shops and pubs and people, not seeing or registering anything. Her mind was a whirl of activity and random thoughts. She had no career, no husband, no life, no chance. She couldn't be a mother, it would be an utter disaster.
Passing the Angel arms pub, she spied a couple sipping beers in the rare April sunshine. Oblivious to others, they mooned at each other, talking quietly. The woman stroked her beau's wrist while he stroked her bare tanned leg absentmindly. They looked as though they lived on their own little orbit, happy and content, comfortable. Cady looked away and kept walking, forcing down the huge lump in her throat. The noise from the traffic eventually pushed its way through her thought pattern, and she realised that she was heading far out of town, and more importantly from the car park her Astra waited in. Probably with a ticket, she had only put two hours on the meter and she could not even bring herself to lift her wrist to look at her watch. Stopping to gain her bearings, she realised she was outside the grey Hepworth Building. A Gallery full of peace and quiet, and beautiful things. Just what she needed to silence the ugly thoughts she was having. Her tummy gurgled, and more importantly, it had a café. She walked over the causeway and entered the Gallery, heading straight to the café. The café itself was even beautiful, and thankfully quiet. A family and a single person were seated. Letting her growling belly do the

ordering she bought a ham, cheese and pickle sandwich, a large coffee, and a huge slice of chocolate cake. She stacked it all up onto a tray and selecting a table overlooking the river, she sat down, staring at the fast moving river and wishing she could float away on it.
"Er..hi!"
Turning to the voice, she looked straight into a pair of huge blue eyes. She had a feeling she knew the owner but…then it clicked.
"Liam, right?"
"Luke actually," the man grinned. "I think I caught you at a bad time the other day, my digits paid the price!" he raised his frankly gorgeous thick manly hands and showed her his fingers, which were now covered in plasters.
"Oh no! I am sorry, er, Luke, it was a bad morning."
He grinned and shrugged. "No problem, I figured you were suffering after a big night on the sauce," he said chuckling, showing off a set of neat white teeth.
Cady stared back at him with a shocked expression. Had he said wrong?
"Er sorry, I meant no offence, it's just that I saw the cards and you looked a bit hungover," he shifted from foot to foot, obviously more uncomfortable by the second. They both stood and stared at each other, the awkwardness nipping at their ankles.
"Birthday was it?" he ventured, trying to save the situation.
Cady smiled at him, amused by his persistence. I bet he wished he hadn't bothered coming over. "I am really sorry about your fingers, and getting your name wrong. Are you ok now?" she said soothingly, reaching for his fingers and stroking the plasters. He jumped slightly in surprise but didn't move his hand away.
Meeting each other's eyes, they both burst into laughter at the weirdness of the situation. Luke smiled and ruffling his slightly messy brown hair, said "Can I join you? I was about to grab a sandwich myself, unless you are waiting for someone?" He looked to the door, as though expecting The Rock to muscle into the room and punch him for talking to his woman.
Cady shook her head. "No, I am not waiting for anyone. I am alone."
Luke nodded and went to get some lunch.

Cady cradled her coffee and took a large gulp. *What the hell was that?* Kissing Marcus, stroking stranger's fingers in galleries, what next, rubbing up against the postman like a bear against a tree? She flushed as Luke turned to stare at her in return and their eyes locked. Man, he had great eyes. She pondered her response as she watched him getting his lunch. She said she was alone. And she was, seemingly. Aside of course, from the little life growing inside her. What was she supposed to do, snuff out the last legacy of a dead man? The baby had done nothing wrong, and she did not think that she could in all honestly even consider an abortion. It was not for her, she had always felt the same. She was pro-choice, and she made her choice sat right there in that café. As Luke passed her a fresh coffee, having noticed hers was cold and had a skin floating on top, she suddenly had a vision of Priscilla in a baby bonnet. She took the mug gratefully and deleted that little horror from her memory banks.

CHAPTER 14

Georgina arrived at the door brandishing the promised goodies, right on time. Cady answered the door chewing a banana, a puzzled faraway look on her face. Scratching her head, creating a comical look akin to an ape, she frowned at George, then her face turned to recognition.
"Oh shit, sorry! I forgot you were coming, come in. Oooh, that curry smells gorge, I am starving."
George kicked off her flats and followed Cady through the hallway into the kitchen. "You ok, mate? How did today go?"
Cady was busy ripping into the two large bags that George had plonked on the table. Spying the two bottles of wine, she whipped them both into the fridge and proceeded to load two plates with curry, shoving a vegetable samosa into her mouth as she piled on the pilau. George stared at her. Something was wrong. Normally Cady would have chosen to sort the wine out first before the food, it was just their way. She knew she had not been taking good care of herself recently, but was this her friend's first meal of the day?
"Have you not eaten today?"
Cady stopped dishing the food out and looked at her mate. "I have actually; I had lunch at the Gallery with a friend."
"Oh, well, are you ok?" George replied, concerned now. Then she remembered. "Oh shit, the clinic! You are not drinking; he gave you something didn't he? What a total skank!"

Cady shook her head vigorously and spoke through a mouthful of chicken dansak. "No, no, he didn't, well not Chlamydia anyway, I got that result back, the rest I have to visit my GP for."
George was confused. She went for regular sexual health checks and she knew that they normally did everything there and then, and even sent a text message with the results when they were available. Not wanting to let her friend know she had such in-depth knowledge, she nodded.
"Everything ok then?" she pushed.
Cady sat down at the island, pushing George's food over to her. Crossing her jean clad legs, she rubbed her bare foot against the

other, a hint of a smile playing on her face. “I’m ok, and I’m pregnant.”
George almost choked on her lamb pasanda. “You’re what! How far gone?”
Cady giggled. “4 months! Can you believe it? I know it’s 4 months, because that’s the only time Richard and I had sex in the last year, so it was kinda easier to do the maths. I looked online and found a due date prediction calendar and I am due near my birthday, the 15th. How weird is that?”
George sat open mouthed, then went to the fridge, uncorked a bottle and took a deep swig, gripping the neck like a wino on a street corner, clutching a bottle of 20/20. Gasping as the alcohol hit her throat and warmed her body, she took a wine glass from the cupboard about Cady and sat back down opposite her. Cady observed her refill her glass and waited for her news to sink in.

It had come as a shock to her too, but now she was kind of excited. She had been talking to Luke and remembering that his firm did extensions, had decided to give the house a makeover, make it her own and she would need a nursery and a play room at the very least. She had no idea what her finances were, she had not even looked at the letter that burned a hole in the spare room carpet under her bed. She just could not face it yet. Tomorrow she would book an appointment with Richard Senior, he would help her, and Luke was scheduled to come round on Friday evening, after he had finished work, he was currently doing a project, but wanted to make a start on her plans. Her tummy flipped at the thought of Luke in her house. She ignored it and turned to George, who was now clutching her wine glass staring back at her.
“Oh Cady, what are you going to do? Do you want me to come with you?”
Cady was grateful for her friend jumping on board.
“Well, I am going to ring the surgery tomorrow and book an appointment with the doctor, and the midwife, I suppose. I imagine that they will need to check the baby, being 4 months already.”
George choked on her wine, banging her teeth against the glass. Spluttering wildly, she whispered “You’re keeping it? Why?”
Cady reeled back, feeling as though she had just had her cheek slapped.

"Of course I am, why wouldn't I?"
George pushed away from her stool, wine sloshing onto the tiles as she gesticulated wildly. "Why! Why! Oh I don't know Cady, sanity, independence? How the hell are you going to cope with a baby, you have just buried your husband and you refuse to deal with that, so how the hell will you process being a mother in 6 months?"
Cady stood up too, anger flashing in her eyes. "5 months, genius, I'm not a friggin' elephant, and how dare you! It's a baby, my baby, what do you want me to do? Suck it out and go back to work, join match.com? Jesus H Christ, why does everyone have an opinion about me and my life? MY husband died, now I am pregnant, MY baby, and I am going to damn well have it! Capesh?"
George stood stock still, wine glass bent, its contents dribbling onto the floor. The drip drip drip of the Zinfandel was the only sound in the room as the two friends glared at each other.
"If you do this Cady, I can't help you, I just can't."
Cady's stomach lurched at her words. Once. Twice. Placing a hand on her only slightly rounded tum, she locked eyes with her childhood companion. She realised, she wasn't jumping on board, she was jumping ship. "Fine. Get out," she spat, "and take your precious vino with you, I am not drinking anymore."
George slammed the wine glass down onto the marble island top, smashing it off the stem. She threw her shoes on in the hallway and slammed the front door behind her.
Cady stared at the broken wine glass, and walking to the sofa, slumped down onto the overstuffed couch, wincing at the discomfort flashing up her back. This sodding couch would the first thing to go. A whole new start. Still resting her hand on her belly, she felt her belly lurch again. A little flutter. She sat still, and it happened again. Oh my god, she thought, it's the baby! She cuddled her not quite there yet bump and whispered, *I'm here little one. It's me and you now, and we will be fine, I promise. Now, fancy a bit of curry and Hugh Grant?*

***

George stood at her Audi door, keys in hand, staring back at Cady's house. Should she go back? She had been such a bitch!

Cady needed support more than ever now, it was just the thought of Cady being saddled alone with a baby, hardly the thing of an independent woman, it was bad enough she married Richard in the first place and turned from a clever full of life girl to a frumpy Stepford wife. What was she going to do now, stop shaving and start wearing head to foot Cath Kidston? Or even worse, talking about the little terror all the time and breastfeeding on the tube wearing a kaftan. Oh Lord, George shuddered, no man will catch her out like that, no chance, rely on no-one and no-one can impose on you. Independence is the only way. She climbed into her Audi and pulled away. She better pack and get some beauty sleep for Paris. Another man waiting for her to work her magic, that was the way she liked it. Being alone was the only way to be. She pulled away from the house and sped off home, Alanis Morrisette banging out of the stereo all the way.

CHAPTER 15

Richard crumpled to the floor, the air crushed out of his lungs by the force of the shock. *Or was it,* he thought*, was he even breathing anymore? At this moment in time, watching his wife talk to her unborn child, their unborn child, he was glad he was dead, because the pain in his chest was killing him now anyway.* Tears escaped his eyes, dripping slowly down his cheeks. Turning to Gerty, his pathetic prone figure, a weepy man in a crumpled suit, made Gerty go to him. Moving her large body surprisingly fluidly, (well, she was an angel) she lowered herself to the floor and held Richard as he cried like a child. He cried for it all, himself, Cady, his parents, and now his child, the child he had never wanted and now, would never see. He cried for all that he would miss out on, and all he could have been. Struggling to control his own grief, he buried his head into Gerty's shoulders, and his body racked with the sobs of despair and loss.

Gerty never said a word, she just held him tight, silently letting her own tears fall. He was a good man, she knew that, and his life was such a waste. Her bosses had obviously chosen not to tell her about the child, and she understood why. Richard's last job was not to do right by the child, he could never do that being dead, it was for them to forgive him, heal the hurt, and help him to cross over. Now it was up to the two of them to form a plan and figure out how to do it. For now though, he needed to keep his anger, they would need his energy. Sensing Richard was spent, she pulled herself away and wiping his tears, she smiled at him kindly.
"Now honey child, we have some work to do. You ready to flash that anger of yours?"

***

Cady walked into the offices of Everett and Stokes with a heady mix of nostalgia, discomfort and fear fizzing through her body, capped off with a nice dose of morning sickness. Since finding out she was pregnant, it was like a switch had been flicked within her, now she had raging morning sickness, breasts that jostled each other angrily for space in her bustier and a neat little baby bump.

Luckily she could conceal it under her suit jacket, and having safety pinned her skirt that morning, she could just about get away with it. For now. She really needed to go maternity shopping. She would have to ask the midwife this afternoon where the best places were. With Georgina being her only real friend outside of work, she had not gleaned much baby info lately.
Walking up to the reception desk she smiled and nodded at Helen, the glamorous but dense receptionist and headed for the lift. Deliberately avoiding her own desk, she headed straight for the office of Richard Senior. Karen smiled broadly at her when she entered the area outside his office, where Karen's desk was situated. She remembered how Richard used to joke that he had her set up so close outside so that she could act like a guard dog against the other partners. Dick was not the sort of person who ever wanted to be disturbed.
"Hi there Cady, how are you doing?" Karen asked, head cocked into the pity pose.

Cady thought for a moment. *'Great thanks, widowed and knocked up'* wasn't quite polite so she simply said, "I am doing ok thanks, day at a time, you know? Is Dick in?"
Karen's face betrayed a flicker of unease. Dick was shouting at someone inside his office, shouting quite loudly actually. And a woman was shouting back at him. Cady shuffled foot to foot uneasily, and pointing to the comfortable regency chair opposite the desk, she sat down and pretended to look for someone in her bag. Damn, if she had her mobile with her, this would be easier.
Suddenly the door to Dick's office flew open, at the same time Priscilla, once again dressed like an sample from DFS, shouted, "I swear it Dick, if you touch her again I will fucking well chop it off!"
Dick strode out after her, mouth poised, one hand reaching for Priscilla's arm in a placating move, when they both noticed Cady sitting there. Cady felt like a child out of bed when she shouldn't be and stood up quickly, grinning like an idiot.
"Hi, I am so sorry to come unannounced; I just wanted a quick word?"

Priscilla turned to Karen and staring right through her barked, "Three coffees please, Karen, if you don't mind scrabbling about after my husband that is." Priscilla then followed this by a hollow laugh, and turning to Dick, murmuring in a low voice like a growling terrier, "Get your mitts off me, Dick. Now."
Cady was horrified by what she just saw. Was Dick having an affair with Karen? Surely not? She suddenly felt a connection to Priscilla, and realised how she must be feeling. She touched her arm lightly. Priscilla flinched and then looking at Cady, fixed her mask of pleasant stiff upper lip in front of her eyes.
"Come in dear, so nice to see you, I assume I can hear this can I?" She put an arm around her and guided her into the office, her look positively steaming when she glared at Dick to move aside. He jumped back quickly, and then hurried to shut the office door.
"You do look pale dear, have you been eating?"

Once they were inside, Dick sat at his desk sheepishly and Priscilla sat in one of the two sofas in the huge office, with Cady selecting the one opposite. They all considered each other for what seemed like forever, till there was a knock at the door. Karen almost broke into a run as she crossed the office floor, head down, and put the elaborately laid tray on the table, complete with Danish pastries, coffee, brown sugar, cream and chocolate mints. As Cady scrutinized her and Dick's behaviour, she realised with a start that it WAS true. They were having an affair. Gazing at Dick now, Cady viewed a totally different person. No wonder Priscilla was so uptight, no wonder she idolised Richard so much, she lived for her son, and since her husband was obviously a cheating arsehole, who could blame her for trying to keep her son close?
Cady realised that Priscilla could have been her future; the only difference was Richard had left her for another woman instead of having his cake and shagging it. Well, she promised herself, that would not be her. This child would be brought up to respect women, and it is was a girl, taught to take no bullshit from the male gender.

Karen continued titivating the tray until Priscilla barked, "I can do that Karen, leave it and piss off, won't you dear?" smiling a perfect

toothy smile as Karen scuttled from the room, closing the door behind her. Karen's face was a picture! Cady had the urge to laugh and air punch at Priscilla's retort, but she sat on her hands to kerb the urge.
Dick cleared his throat and spoke, obviously to clear the knives slashing about him from the air. "So Cady dear, how are you? You wanted a word?"
Cady took a deep breath and looked at her in-laws in turn. "I really just wanted to ask, my financial situation now, er, what is it? Do I need to return to work? Richard dealt with everything, I just paid for the food really, so I don't really have the first idea about what I owe."
Cady shook her head mentally at herself. She sounded pathetic, '*please Sir, can I have some more housekeeping?*' Before she met Richard, she had her own house, mortgage, and commuted everywhere, paid her own bills and wiped her own arse. How the mighty had fallen.
Dick was looking confused. "Did the letter from Richard not explain everything?"
Cady grimaced, sucking the air in through her clenched teeth. "I haven't opened it, I..can't, not yet."
Dick nodded. "Well basically Cady darling, Richard was very careful with the planning, the house is paid for, all the utilities are up to date and paid, and all his debts have been paid for, not that he had any other than the car and credit cards. So the money in his account has been transferred to yours, and you have the entirety of the joint account, you will get his pension, and the life insurance left you with a sizeable chunk too. Basically my dear, if you are careful you will never have to work again. Have you been using the car? It really does need a run out, a car like that. You really do need to read that letter though, darling, that explains all the figures."
Cady let his words sink in. She was financially secure. Wow, that was a relief. She smiled and rubbed her tummy. *We will be ok, bubs.*
Dick brought her back to the room. "Cady, dear, the car? Have you driven it recently?"
Cady thought of Richard's black Mercedes C250 Coupe. His pride and joy. He had always ribbed her car, joshing that she was not fit

to park next to his car on the drive, and should park on the street round the corner. Her Astra was a bit battered, but it was paid for in full, all by herself and she was proud of that fact.
"I haven't no, it's not at home, it's here."
Dick shook his head. "It isn't dear, security would have told me, and I haven't seen it either. I assumed he had left it at home."
Cady remembered he had had a drink that night, hence the cab. Ironically, it wasn't even the same cab that knocked him down.
"No Dick, it's not at home. I have his keys here, they were on him when…."
Priscilla nodded, speaking suddenly, "Give us the keys dear, I will contact the police, they will find the car. Let us deal with it, you have enough on."
Cady nodded. "I don't want the car, so if you want it.."
Priscilla and Dick both shook their heads together in a reverse nodding dog like fashion. "We couldn't either, Cady, don't worry, we will sell it and send you the money. That ok?"
Cady nodded, grateful to have that matter taken from her. She picked up her oversized bag and searched for the keys. Man, this bag needed a clean out. Rustling through scrunched up papers, balled up tissues and stray mints, she proceeded to pull things out, still rooting for the keys. Priscilla gasped suddenly, and pointing to the scattered contents said, "Cady, are you on drugs?"
Cady's head whipped up. Following Priscilla's shocked wide eyes, she spotted what had given her cause for concern. Nestled amongst the Gallery leaflets and snot rags, was a urine sample sealed in a clear plastic sandwich bag. The sample she did this morning, for the midwife that afternoon.
"Well, are you? Is that why you need clean urine, to dodge rehab tests or something? Dick, she is on drugs! Do you see? I saw a Panorama program about this!"
Realising that she was about to talk about the perils of needle sharing and whiteys Cady blurted out, "I am not on drugs, Priscilla. I'm pregnant. And yes, it's Richard's baby, and yes I am keeping it. The urine is for my midwife."
Priscilla crumpled then, knees hitting the floor. "Oh no, oh no, oh no," she said, over and over. Dick went to her awkwardly, not daring advance for fear of her swatting him. Cady tutted at him and kneeled down next to Priscilla.

"Priscilla, I know that you are sad, I am too, but this baby is half Richard, and you are, and always will be its' grandmother. I would never stop you being a part of our lives, if that's what you are worrying about."
Priscilla snorted loudly and grabbing Cady, yanked her into a death grip. "Oh thank you, thank you! You don't know what this means to me, a whole new life, oh what a miracle, thank you!"
Cady nodded, or tried to, with Priscilla crushing her.
"I am glad you are happy, but can you let me go? The little miracle you are referring to is doing the stomp on my poor bladder at the minute."

CHAPTER 16

Georgina stomped confidently in the plush Parisian offices of Marshall and Marshall and marched right up to the desk, flashing her credentials at the very glamorous receptionist. Within minutes George was sat in a huge office sipping coffee, facing a window wall looking out at the beautiful scenery. The weather was crisp and clear, not bad for June in Paris. She decided to take the rare moment to savour the country she was in for a change. Taking off her heels and rubbing her stockinged feet, she padded over to the window and rubbing her toes in the plush deep pile, she stretched her arms out wide and took a huge breath.
"One day, I shall come to visit and actually spend time with you," she murmured wistfully to the skyline. Sighing, she dropped her arms, and straightening herself, whirled around. Three men were stood beside the open door, staring at her questioningly. Two of the men looked at each other quizzically and took her seats, declaring to each other in French that they thought she was quite mad. Which would be fine, except that George understood every word, being able to speak fluent French and Spanish. The third guy hovered there and as she took her seat, she peeked a glance at him. Suddenly glad she was sitting down, she cleared her throat and hands shaking, opened her briefcase to take out her paperwork. WOW. This man was gorgeous. Stood in a designer black suit and skinny black tie, (obviously Armani, this season, shoes, Dolce and Gabbana, also this season) he was the typical tall, dark and handsome man. Except this guy was also dipped in gorgeous sauce and smothered in hotty topping. Geez. George felt her body getting warmer by the second, and smoothing her suddenly damp palms on her jacket, she struggled to gain control. Mr Armani took his seat, and waited in silence. She straightened her papers and sat. Sat grinning like an utter idiot. The silence palpable now, the two other men, carbon copies of each other and significantly older than their companion, again looked at each other with a look of confusion. Then he spoke up.
"So Miss Elliot, is it? Are you ready to start our meeting?"

Georgina, ridiculously grateful for him breaking the ice, nodded and smiled, willing her body to stop acting like a lunatic teenager.
Pull it together woman!
She spied a smirk on his face. Was he laughing at her? She remembered her performance at the window. Oh Christ, he thinks I am an idiot, oh great, and now I am proving that point by staring him like an imbecile. Standing up abruptly, she pulled out her laptop and starting it up, began to click into professional mode. Passing over handouts, she got to work making her presentation, all the while aware that he was watching her with an amused smirk on his face. George's first thought was that he was arrogant, and slightly annoying. Second thought was what he looked like under that shirt.
Finally the presentation was at an end. The French equivalent of Tweedledum and Tweedledee were now much happier, nodding in agreement at each other. Satisfied, they shook hands with George, explained pleasantries and wandered off for lunch.
Left in the room alone now, she started to pack her things away and fired off an e-mail on her Blackberry to her boss telling him she had the contract squared away and was starting the IT package immediately. Tapping her phone, she then thought of Cady. They had not spoken in days and she hated how things had been left. Firing off a quick text, she simply put SO SORRY XX BACK IN A MONTH, PLS TALK 2 ME.
Frowning, she hit send and stared at her phone. She probably hadn't even switched her mobile on yet.
"Bad day?"
George smiled wryly and looked straight at him. He had the nicest brown eyes, framed with short black hair and the slight signs of stubble on his well chiselled face. Gerard Butler, eat your heart out.
"Something like that, yes." Locking her suitcase, she made for the door.
"I'm Ben by the way. Great work today, you nailed it. Fancy some lunch?"
George opened her mouth to decline, but thought better of it. She only normally ate in the hotel, plane or from the curled up buffets the offices provided, maybe he would at least suggest a café.
"Yes, that would be great thanks, and call me Georgina."

***

Cady closed her front door behind her and sagged against it. The midwife had gone well, she was doing fine and had even heard the baby's heartbeat, which in itself was an emotional experience. She was just glad she had managed to talk Priscilla out of accompanying her to the appointment, she needed to get her own head around developments without her exuberant mother-in-law in tow. She had just about ran out of the office, promising to phone regularly with updates. Richard Senior had patted her on the shoulder, murmuring gruffly, "I hope it's a little Dick you have in there." It was all Cady could do to keep a straight face. She had squeezed his hand and nodded instead, biting the sides of her mouth to prevent a bout of hysteria popping out.

George would have howled at that one. Remembering that they were not speaking, Cady sighed and plodded up the stairs. Nap time, definitely nap time. Thank god it was Friday, she could spend the weekend hiding away in peace. Just when she neared the top of the stairs, there was a knock at the door. Bugger. Bending down to peek at the caller, she saw a man's silhouette through the frosted glass pane. She went to open the door. Marcus was stood there, all jumpy and nervous. The huge bouquet of Calla lilies he was carrying were vibrating, sending a waft of scent straight up her nostrils. Man, this pregnancy had turned her into a bloodhound. Over the scent of the flowers, she could smell Marcus's aftershave. The combination was not entirely unpleasant.
"Er hi," she ventured awkwardly, "would you like to come in?"
Marcus bolted inside. Cady frowned and shutting the door, turned to him and saw that he had dropped the flowers and striding close to her, he pulled her into his arms. Burrowing his slender fingers into her hair, pulling it free from the loose knot, he grabbed her and kissed her. And kissed, kissed, kissed her. Forcefully, urgently at first and then tenderly and slowly, he explored her mouth passionately, all the time running one hand through her hair and grasping her neck with the other. Cady kissed him back just as urgently and as he moved his hand lower over her body, to grasp her sides tightly, she stopped and broke free from the kiss. Panting, Marcus reached for her hand and rubbing her palm for her thumb, said softly, "I'm sorry, I just had to kiss you. Cady, I know that this

is wrong and very, very bad timing, not to mention hideously appropriate, but I have wanted to do that for the longest time, and after the other day, I just had to come back and do it again."
His eyes crinkled and Cady saw pain etched on his flushed face. He patted his palm over his heart. "You're in here, Cady, always have been, it's killing me to see you in so much pain, but this is it. Make or break, as the saying goes, I am here. For you. I expect nothing."
He looked stricken and dragging his palms against his face, said, "I offer you everything. When and if you want it."
Cady was still processing his words when she heard the door click behind her, the flowers on the floor the only proof of what had just occurred. The uneventful Friday afternoon nap was not to happen for Cady.

CHAPTER 17

As the taxi pulled away from the restaurant, Georgina placed her handbag on her lap and almost hugged it. She was so happy! Dinner had been amazing, she had had a wonderful time. Ben was not only gorgeous, but also attentive and funny and the conversation had not stopped once. Born in London, Ben had moved to Paris for work five years ago, and now at 35 he was the youngest CEO the company had ever had. He knew his stuff too, it was nice not to have to dumb herself down with him as they talked about their careers. Georgina was used to men eating out of her hands personally and professionally, but normally when she started telling them about the work they had employed her to do, their eyes either glazed over or descended to her chest for the rest of the exchange. Ben however, was interested and seems to understand a bit about IT himself. George had found herself aroused mentally and physically and also, if she had to admit it, he made her a little nervous. Not terrified nervous, but nerve zingingly nervous, excitement fizzing through her body at the proximity of him. It was new, and it did scare her, but like any other drug, she wanted more. And as she sped back to her hotel to get changed to meet him for the evening, she fully intended to enjoy her time in Paris for once. Turning off the independent voice in her head telling her to get a grip, she mentally perused her suitcase for something to wear. Damn, as usual, she had packed for all business all the time. Hmmm, luckily the hotel was a small French boutique one, so with any luck she could pick up something new from there. And maybe even some new perfume. And shoes to match, or course….and she might even pick up some new underwear too….George continued to hug her bag, grinning like an idiot at the prospect her night out presented.

***

Cady was dressed in sweat pants and a baggy pink t-shirt when the doorbell rang. Her hair in a messy loose bun, she blew a wisp away from her eyes and answered the door awkwardly in her rubber gloves. Standing there with a very confused look and a bottle of wine was Luke.
"Er, hiya, did you forget our appointment?"

Cady looked at herself, and then back at her house. She had started a cleaning frenzy, currently the contents of all her cupboards were scattered across the kitchen and the smell of cleaning products was quite pungent.
"Sorry, I did actually, come in." Cady moved aside for Luke to enter, suddenly very aware that she was dressed as a scruff and had a fine sheen of sweat on her skin. Motioning for Luke to sit on the couch, he smiled and passed her the wine.
"I know it's late, but happy birthday anyway!"
Cady took the wine. *Birthday, what was he talking about?*
"Er right, thanks…er, would you like a glass? I just need to have a quick shower if you don't mind."
Luke stood up, taking the wine back. "It's ok, you go, I'll sort the wine out."
Cady nodded and dashed upstairs to the bedroom, stripping off her sweats and throwing them into the basket behind her. Grabbing some fresh underwear, she pulled out a pair of jeans and a cute white sweater and dashed to the bathroom, shutting the master bedroom door behind her.

Ten minutes later, she was back downstairs. She felt fresher but suddenly tired. To her surprise, Luke was sat watching TV with a glass of wine in his hand. The scene of him sitting on the couch was oddly familiar and comforting and Cady chose to sit beside him on the couch. Luke, not hearing her come in was startled and nearly dropped his glass.
"Sorry," Cady chuckled. "Are you o- oh, oh….ouch!"
She was suddenly bent in half on the sofa, sharp pains stabbing her in the stomach. Jesus Christ, this hurt…
Luke hurriedly put his wine down on the coffee table and knelt by her feet.
"Are you ok?"
Cady was scared, and in pain. The baby….
"No I think I need to go to the hospital, I'm four months pregnant."
Luke had taken her hand by now and his grip suddenly tightened.
"You're what?"
"I'm pregnant! This hurts, can you please get me to a hospital!"
Luke ran for the phone.

"The phone's dead, there's no dial tone! Have you got a mobile, I left mine at the office."
Luke cursed himself for leaving his phone locked in his desk. Truth was, with his ex constantly bothering him with so called 'work calls,' he had been jolly well glad to leave it.
Meanwhile, Cady was cursing herself for cutting the phone off her landline and hiding her mobile. It would be flat now, anyway.
"Have you got a car? Can you drive me there?" Cady looked at him imploringly. The pains were shooting up and down her stomach now, making it rock hard. She was tensed up with pain and sweating quite a bit now with panic and alarm.
Luke visibly paled.
"Oh fucking hell, I came on my push bike! Have you got a car, where are your keys?"
He pulled her to her feet, letting her put her full weight against him.
"Ow, ow, ow…there in the door with the house ones."
"Fine, fine," Luke said, pulling her coat around her as they headed for the door. "I only had two sips of wine, I'll drive, ok?"
Cady nodded and gripped his arm. "Liam, I'm scared, I don't want to lose my baby."
Luke cradled her head to his shoulder.
"It will be fine I promise, let's just get you there and get checked out."
Walking her out into the cool starlit night as though she were fine china, he lowered her into the passenger seat and raced round to the driver side. Belting himself and her up, he edged the Astra out and drove as fast as he could to the hospital, jaw set the whole way. At every red light, he placed his hand on hers, as she rested hers on the bump. Neither of them spoke till they reached the reception desk at the hospital, where Luke rather masterfully demanded a wheelchair and a doctor, his deep voice booming across the corridors, sending the hospital staff running. Cady, in shock and grateful for a fast drive, grabbed Luke's hand again and held it as they wheeled her off. *Little did they know, above them Richard had turned every light from red to green, using his energy to try and help his unborn child. Gerty watched him commanding the traffic, passion in his urgent actions, concentration on his face. He was starting to get why he was here.*

Having been checked over by the nurse and her blood pressure taken, Cady was settled onto a bed and advised to wait for the doctor. She had a feeling it wouldn't be long, given the fuss that Luke had kicked up in reception. Even through her pain she wanted to laugh at him screaming at the staff, telling them to get their arses in gear and threatening legal action. It was really cute actually, in a non arrogant way, Richard had always been an arrogant man to be out with, he normally only kicked off when his car was not valeted properly or his fillet mignon was not prepared to his exact tastes.
Now laid on the hospital bed, she was so glad she had showered and changed out of her sweats. The pains had subsided now, and she felt a little less panicked than before. She was not bleeding so that was a blessing too. She rubbed her tiny bump and looked across at Luke who was sitting in the chair next to her. His expression was pure panic.
"Liam, thank you, I feel a little better now. The nurse said she doesn't think it's serious, and I-"
Luke jumped in, pulling his chair right up to the bed. "How does she know? They haven't even examined you yet, it's ridiculous, shall I go complain again?"
Cady laughed. "Liam, it's fine, I promise."
"Cady," he said, frowning. "My name is Luke, not Liam."
She groaned. "Oh god, I am so sorry! I keep doing that don't I!"
Luke batted her apologies away. "It's fine, don't worry. Now please, can I call someone, your husband, is he working away?"
Cady grabbed his hand and placed it against her bump. "Luke, it's kicking, can you feel it?"

Luke gasped as her belly bounced against his palm. He could feel something wiggling around under his palm, it was so weird!
"Oh wow! See, little one's a fighter," he said, beaming at her.
Looking at Cady, he suddenly felt more than the baby. Forcing himself to push the thought away, he tried again.
"Have you got a number for your husband? I can call him, or your mother?"
Cady's grin slid from her face. "I don't have anyone really. My parents and I are not close, I can't stand them to be honest, and my husband, well he died, two months ago."

She looked at him sadly, and he thought his pumping heart would betray him against the silence of the ward. He had an urge to protect her, it was so strong he had to stop himself from kissing her there and then. Instead he settled for stroking her fingers as they both lay entwined on her bump.
"That's why I wanted you to come and do the house. I need a new home, for me and the little wotsit here, we need a new life."
Luke squeezed her hand. "Well you came to the right place, little wotsit," he said to the bump, "because making plans are my speciality."

***

Richard flopped onto the pure white floor, exhausted from the energy outburst. Gerty sat and watched him as always. When he turned to her, she smiled at him.
"Do you see now, my child?"
Richard sighed. "I see that I am dead, and that my wife is having my child, but how am I to help? Flick a few traffic lights, is that it? Or am I being punished, by being made to watch?"
Gerty got to her feet and walked away. Richard saw that she was walking to another vision, this time of his parents' house.
"Richard, if you were being punished, I think that they would have sent you somewhere a bit hotter, do you understand?"
He shuddered and nodded. "Ok so what then? Just tell me what I have to do."
Gerty pointed to the vision, which had now changed to his father and mother arguing.
"You already know what you have to do. Everything else will fall into place."
Richard got to his feet and strode towards the vision. His parents were arguing again, and as Richard listened, he got the shock of his life. Dad was cheating again, but this time Priscilla was leaving. His parents were splitting up! He knew now that he had to help, Jesus, he sure had thrown his life away having affairs and now it seemed his father was finally going to pay for his own activities. They needed each other, he just had to show them that and hope it wasn't too late.
Priscilla picked up Dick's golf trophy and hurled it at him. Dick ducked and groaned as it hit his favourite painting. Grabbing

another item, this time a flower vase, complete with flowers, she glared at Richard, eyes wild and rage pulsing through her.
"You utter bastard! You promised me never again!!! I am such a fool! And now our boy is dead, and we have a grandchild on his way, and you still can't stop sticking it to the staff! Arrghhh!"
Grunting she drew back the vase and threw it with all her might. Their faces both dropped as they saw it was heading for one of Richard's art pieces just put up in their home. Just as the vase was about to make contact however, it stopped. Stopped and hovered, and then placed itself on the side table nearby. Dick and Priscilla ran to each other, frightened to death. *Did that vase just move by itself?*
Clinging together, their argument forgotten, they both started as the CD player sprang into life, playing Moon River. *Their wedding song?* Priscilla stepped away from Dick and shaking, whispered "Richard?"
She gasped as a photo frame fell to the floor. Without going to it, she knew what it was, a picture of them in Margate many years ago, their happy smiling faces turned to the camera laughing as Richard sat in between them, ice-cream all over his pudgy baby cheeks.
Dick enveloped Priscilla in a hug, and they both crumpled to the floor, cradling the photo. It was Richard, they knew it. As Moon River played on repeat, they started to talk and several tear stained hours later, as they danced to the music, swaying together, they felt him leave the room.

***

Cady woke up in hospital, and looking around her, she realised that she was not alone. Luke was propped up in the chair next to her, his hand still placed on hers. The pains had stopped now. She sat up quietly, not wanting to wait Luke, and reaching to the bedside cabinet with her right hand, picked up the black and white photo that held an image of her future.
The little blob on the picture looked like nothing really, but to her it was everything, and she couldn't put into words the rush of love she had felt when she first saw the jiggling shape on the screen. Luke had stayed too, and did not even bat an eye when the sonographer called him daddy, he just smiled and flushed.

Obviously to spare my embarrassment, she thought. What was he going to say, 'actually I am just her builder, her husband's a cheating corpse?' Cady put the photo back and looked at him. He was really cute, and even in sleep he had the same worried expression he had had all night, since he had returned from picking up some clothes for them both from their homes. She was still staring at him when his phone rang in his pocket, breaking the peace of the moment. Luke jumped and surprisingly ignored his phone.
"Hi, you ok? My phone didn't wake you, did it?"
How cute was that, he was all concern. Cady smiled. "Nope, I was awake, listen if you have to be somewhere, it's fine you know, the doctor said it was just normal stretching pains, the baby's fine."
Luke was already shaking his head. "No. They said you can go home today, I will take you home, and if you are up to it, we can look at the plans there, I need to make some adjustments for the baby anyway, so we might as well get on with it, unless you have changed your mind?"
Cady sat up. "No, I want to get cracking, make that house ours. Er, mine and the baby, I mean."
Luke grinned. "Good, I will just see about some breakfast then, eh? Some juice or something? I could smuggle in some rubber pancakes from McDonalds if you like."
Her stomach gurgled. "That sounds amazing, please."
"Cool, I will be right back ok? Are you sure I can't call anyone?"
She thought for a moment. George was still in Paris and she hated babies anyway, so that was out. Her in-laws would go into meltdown. Things were awkward with Marcus still, and he didn't even know about the baby. Her own parents were a definite no-go.
"Nope, no-one just yet. I will probably call them when I get home."
Luke nodded. "Pancakes it is then."

***

Victoria slammed down the phone, a hissy fit brimming and zinging on her nerve endings. Bloody Luke! Not answering the phone to her now, that was pathetic! He would have known it was her too, with her own extension number. And now it was after nine and he was still not in. What gives? She knew it would be difficult,

a challenge even, to get him back but she never expected him to be so cold and indifferent. He used to eat from the palm of her hand, but now he would not even spare **her** the crumbs on his plate!
As usual, Victoria was oblivious to her own failings. Wiping from her memory completely the fact that he walked in on her shagging his university roommate, she thought of herself as the perfect girlfriend. She had made a beeline for Luke, right from fresher's' week. She had scoped him out and got the measure of him in seconds. Some people were good at collecting antiques, or were arty, or literary minded, but not Victoria. Although she was a very clever, sharp, highly talented architect, she used her powers for evil, not good. Her ability was men. Rooting them out, using them, profiting from them, and then getting out without a cross word or a blot on her reputation. She was a ball buster, heartbreaker and bank balance decimator, all wrapped up in one cute little package.
Luke had always been different though. He was not a fool, and she had had to work for a change to land him as her boyfriend. Trouble was though, once she won her challenge, she lost interest and inevitably, started to hump someone's leg like an overexcited terrier. But now, two years after they broke up, she still couldn't quite get him out of her head. She was bored with bed hopping and the attention she got from men had lost its shine somehow. So here she was, working with Luke and desperate to make him love her again. Except, if he wasn't in the office, or answering his phone, it would be pretty impossible to crack his hard shell. Still, his dad liked her, she had an ally there. Adjusting her cleavage so that it was more precariously placed in her bra, she slicked on some lip gloss and sashayed to her desk to put a plan into action. She would make herself indispensable and push her way into Luke's life, work, and eventually heart.

CHAPTER 18

Marcus's door slammed, causing the glass to vibrate. Marcus stopped talking, phone still in hand and stared at Angela. Man, Friday night! He had forgotten. Angela strode over to the desk and grabbed the receiver out of his hand, replacing it into the cradle with a quiet click.
"You were not there on Friday. I specifically told you where to come, I left a note and a message with your secretary. Just what do you think you are playing at, Marcus?"
Marcus was aghast. Not to mention the scene she made coming into his office, she had also just put the phone down on an important client. He had no excuse, he had just gone home after Cady's on Friday, showered and drunk beer into the early hours, a pity party of sorts, relief that he had told Cady how he felt, and dread and fear about what her reaction would be. It now being Monday, and having still not heard a peep from her, he was guessing that the news wasn't good.
Angela's perfectly threaded eyebrows were arched high now, lips pursed at his obvious lack of grovelling, apology, or movement at all.
"I have to tell you something, I don't want to discuss it here, so after work, come to mine please. It can't wait. I won't be ignored, Marcus, so just deal with it."
She pivoted on her Manolos and thundered back to her office, slamming the door on its already screaming hinges.
Sighing, he slung his office chair back. *Great,* he thought. *In love with my dead best friend's wife, and meanwhile I have Glenn Close careening round the office, bunny in hand.*

Determined to change his fortunes, or at least get a final answer, he dialled Cady again. The mobile had been switched off since Richard's death, and the land line just rang out, but it was still worth a try. After Cruella had said her peace that evening, he fully intended to swing by Cady's on his way home.
"Hello?"
A man's voice answered Cady's phone. Marcus for a second thought it was Richard, and then felt his heart plummet slightly

when he remembered. A mix of relief and guilt, and sorrow that his mate was really gone.
"Er..hello? Is Cady home please?"
Luke whispered into the phone. "She is asleep upstairs, but who is it calling? Are you a friend, I could use some help…"

***

Priscilla stiffened as she passed Richard, sat at the telephone table in the hall. The police had found Richard's car. She was dusting anyway so could move around easily and earwig as she worked, floral apron tied over her simple skirt and blouse. Dick had taken some time off from the office so they could work on their marriage, but it being only the first working day, they were still skirting around each other, unsure of how to deal with their new dynamic.
Having had years of him working long hours and Priscilla raising Richard and running the home, when Richard left Priscilla was crippled with empty nest syndrome. After all, when you put your life into being a wife and mother, what happens when no-one depends on you anymore? Dick was never there, and save for cooking his tea and ironing his shirts, he never noticed her either. She could have pulled a naked chef number off, boobies a go-go over the stove and he would still have paid more attention to his beef bourguignon.
As she brushed the yellow duster over her knick-knacks, listening to the phone, she was relieved by what she heard. Richard's car had been found parked up safe and sound, quite nearby, next to a modern apartment block. Priscilla pondered this information. Georgina had said that Richard was leaving Cady that evening, it must have been his new place. Dick replaced the receiver and looked across at his wife.
"The police are happy for us to remove the car since we have the keys and are next of kin. It has a fair few tickets that will need dealing with, apparently. We can drive it back here, get the garage to collect it and deal with the sale."
Looking at her husband, she pulled her coat from the rack in the hallway. "Do you think that he had an apartment there?"
Dick nodded.

"I was wondering the same thing, maybe they have a reception, those new flash apartment blocks usually do these days, doormen and the like. Let's go for a walk first eh, before I go get it? I need a bit of fresh air first I think."
Pulling her coat around her, she headed to the door, her husband in tow. They were both silent on the walk, neither really wanting to undertake the task in hand. It was set to be another difficult week.

***

Cady awoke to the smell of fresh bacon. Her tummy gurgled and groaned under the freshly washed fragrant covers. Propped up in bed supported by a huge mass of pillows, she felt like the Queen of Sheba. Luke had brought her home that Saturday morning and had not left since, choosing instead to sleep on the sofa. He was like Mrs Mop, doing her shopping, washing her bed sheets, cooking, cleaning, and generally keeping her company. To be honest, she was so tired and depleted of everything that she had just let him. She had pretty much slept for the entire weekend, and now she must admit to feeling pretty great. Hungry for the smells wafting from her kitchen, she swung her legs out of the spare room bed and reached for her robe, which Luke had also washed and hung on the back of the door. She walked to the bathroom, glancing at the closed master bedroom door. She really would have to open that door sometime and sort out the other rooms too, after all, she had a baby coming soon, and there was a lot of work to be done before then. Grimacing at the cold bathroom tiles, she opened the cabinet to search for a tie for her hair. She did look better, still pale, but she looked rested at least. Living in bed for the past couple of days had not done her hair any favours though, her blonde hair was a tangle of loops and swirls, stuck at right angles all over her head. She ran a comb through it as best she could and scraped it into a clip at one side of her head. Better than it was. A quick brush of the teeth and she started to float downstairs to the aroma of breakfast. Halfway down the stairs and she could hear Luke talking. *Was someone here?*
"Victoria, I told you, stop bloody calling me! I don't work for you, remember, Dad knows where I am, I can work from here, so just…what? Oh Victoria, seriously?"

Cady stopped at the kitchen alcove, suddenly feeling like an intruder on the conversation. *Who was Victoria? Client? Didn't sound like a client. He wasn't married, surely? He had been here all weekend!*
Luke was furiously shaking his head at the caller on the phone, obviously disagreeing with her rant, and it was a rant and a half, Cady could tell that much from her tiny tinny tones, carried from the mobile around the room. Luke sat down at the breakfast stool, swigging from a cup on the counter. He looked so..at home here, it was strange, Richard had never looked that relaxed, and he had been minus a nut job phone conversation. Luke made an unexpected fast hand gesture at the phone, causing Cady to erupt with laughter. Definitely his wife then.

***

Looking at her son's car, Priscilla felt her heart do its regular imploding thing. She actually felt her organ skip a couple of beats, as though momentarily giving up, remembering that her only child had gone forever, and deciding that pumping blood in that moment was not worth the effort, like how other people felt about cleaning their windows or going to church. Grasping Dick's hand tighter, she covered her heart with her other palm. Today had not been a good day. Having discovered where Richard's car was, Dick had gone to retrieve it, pocketing their son's keys and hailing a cab. Priscilla wondered why all the secrecy, till she read the address on the telephone pad. Scribbled down in Dick's own script was an address, not of Richard's supposed new flat it seemed, but of an address they both knew, and had in fact visited before. For an afternoon barbeque, of a person at work. A woman, no less. So Richard hadn't got a flat on his own, he had simply moved in with someone else, right from his wife's bed to another's. To say that he was a chip off the block was a heart shattering understatement. Priscilla ripped the paper from the pad and folding it primly in two, she placed it into her apron pocket and smoothed back her hair, ever the vision of immaculate perfection, feelings firmly put back in check.
This would not be the last of it, she knew that much.
The visit they had witnessed together had changed them as a couple, made them realise that they needed to pull it together or rip it asunder once and for all, for their sakes and for the memory of

their son, and they had chosen to fight one last time for each other and their marriage. Finally forsaking all others on Dick's part. Shame they had not realised it sooner; they had taught their only son the basics of living, appreciating the finer things in life, working hard, studying hard, achieving all, never having to struggle in life, but they never taught him how to be a man, a good man at least. Priscilla walked to her lounge dresser and gazed at the silver polished frames scattered across the surface. Richard from baby to independent being. His smiling face peered at her from mountain peaks, office desks, fire truck toys, and the church he got married in. Picking up the wedding frame, she thumbed the picture of Cady. The poor girl was going through so much, and her anger was penting everything up. She was acting like she herself had, the wronged wife, not the grieving widow. The rage was the cork in her emotions, stopping her from mourning Richard's passing. And if everything came out, it would only get worse. So much worse. They had to find a way to help her. Picking up her bag, she walked out of the front door, trying her best not to throw herself on her son's car and sob out her heart.

***

Marcus knocked at the door, flowers in hand, to be faced by a harassed looking Luke, dressed in a white shirt, blue jeans and bare feet. He had a cup of coffee in his hand and a pencil behind his ear.
"Hello, Marcus right? Come in please."
Marcus was stunned momentarily, not for the first time that evening, and allowed himself to be shepherded into the lounge. Blueprints and plans covered every available space, apart from the couch, which held a very pale but smiling Cady, wrapped in a dressing gown and duvet. He perched on the couch next to her as Luke tried to do the same. Luke grinned at Cady knowingly.
"Coffee, Marcus?"
Marcus scowled at him irritably.
"Yes, two sugars and milk. Please," he replied, practically spitting the last word at Luke's retreating back. He lowered his voice.
"Cady, what's going on? Who is this guy? He answers your mobile, your door, asks me to come 'visit'?"
Cady smiled and sat up, stretching out her legs to the floor.

"Luke is my architect and builder. I am remodelling the house. I'm pregnant Marcus, and I am keeping it. I had a funny turn and Luke was….just there, luckily."
Marcus stared at her in disbelief. His mouth was drying out, he could feel it, his tongue a hollowed husk rattling around his dusty cavern. He put the flowers done on top of a stack of papers.
"I have no right to ask, but us?"
Cady looked down.
"Marcus, my husband destroyed my faith in men. Now he is dead, and you were his best friend, and with the baby coming, it's just not going to happen.."
She looked at him through hooded lids. Truth was, she wanted him to fight for her. She did not want to do this alone. And he was nice, he loved her, maybe it would work….
"Cady, I told you how I feel. That hasn't changed."
He looked her straight in the eye, and started to say something else.
"But…I.."
Cady looked away.
"See, it wouldn't work, I told you, it's fine."
Hearing Luke returning, Marcus cupped her chin in his hand and grabbing a quick kiss, he whispered urgently.
"Cady, we will make it work, meet me tomorrow, 1 o'clock, in the park?"
Cady breathed out slowly, taking in his words.
"Ok," she whispered back.
Luke, hearing their conversation, slapped on an innocent smile and passed out the coffees. So, Marcus was going to swoop in was he? *We will see, mate, I am here for a while yet,* he thought to himself. Marcus was a flyboy, a suit, a player, he knew it from the off. Slow and steady wins the race Lukey boy. And now he had chance to know Cady, he was in this race for the long haul.
They chatted awkwardly for a while, mostly Cady and Luke telling Marcus about the plans for the extension and the remodel. The house would be like brand new, and work was due to start next month, once the plans had been finalised and the house prepared. No one spoke of the rooms with the closed doors and the possessions behind them, that would have to be dealt with very soon. Cady couldn't face the thought, she wished that they could just remove the rooms entirely and start again. Still, she would

have to tackle it sometime, and she would need help. Asking Luke seemed too weird. Maybe she would ask Marcus to help her tomorrow, that would still be weird, but he knew Richard, and the only other alternative was his parents, and Priscilla was still adjusting to life after son, she couldn't put that on her.
Marcus left soon after; citing an early start at work, but Cady could tell he looked tired and a bit stressed. Thinking it was work being busy with Richard gone, she didn't mention it to him. They would talk tomorrow.
When he had gone, Luke locked up and sat on the sofa with her.
"Luke, you know, I am fine now, and you do have a life. I can't ask you to live on my couch forever, I am fine really."
Putting his hands on hers, they both stared at the fire in silence. They both felt so comfy and relaxed, they sat there a while before anyone spoke.
"A couple more nights, for my own peace of mind. And I love your couch, it's not a hard task. Ok?" Luke looked at her nervously; begging her with his eyes to let him stay a bit longer to protect her, make sure she was ok. He could not bear to think of her in this house of locked doors and ghosts.
Cady smiled back at him, relieved he had not taken the out just yet. His wife must be understanding, or did she just not care?
"Ok, thanks."
Returning their gazes to the fire, they sat arm in arm till they both fell asleep.

Richard, watching the pair, half smiled to Gerty.
"Think he will be a good dad to my baby?" he whispered, his voice cracking.
Gerty touched his shoulder.
"If it's meant to be, it will be. We just have to help it along a little, when we can. You ok with this?"
Richard kept his gaze on the sleeping couple.
"He is everything I never was to her. They are more relaxed with each other in a few days than we were in years. I can live with it. Or rest in peace with it," He chuckled at his own joke.

CHAPTER 19

Georgina sat on the toilet, her feet scrunched up, toes clinging to each other against the harsh cold of the white bathroom tiles. Manoeuvring herself while semi hovering over the toilet, she tutted loudly as she managed to pee on her hand. Placing the stick on top of her laundry basket perched on about half a roll of toilet paper, she pulled up her knickers and washed her hands thoroughly, scrubbing till her hands were pink and sore. Resting on the edge of the bath, she covered her head in her hands and listened to Magda shuffling around outside the door.

"Do you vant coffee this morning? I am making, yes?"

George opened the door and looked at Magda, balancing a pile of fluffy towels in her arms. Taking them from her, she stuffed them into the airing cupboard and nodded.

Coffee would be great, thanks."

George saw Magda's eyes fall onto the pregnancy test. Magda nodded towards it. "You look yet?"

George shook her head, suddenly terrified to move. "No. Will you?"

Magda nodded and patting her on the shoulder, she walked past and peered at the stick, picking up the box and reading the instructions at the back, and looking at the test again. She put the box down and turned to her.

"We need coffee now. We talk first, then I tell. Yes?"

George frowned. What? Magda gave her no time to answer, wrapping the stick up in the tissue, she walked into the kitchen and putting the test out of reach, she poured the coffee.

"So tell me, you want baby? Father know?" She sat at the table, gesturing for her to sit down.

George sat down numbly. She took a big swig of coffee and spoke. She really talked, too. About her feelings of abandonment from her parents, her need for stability and independence, the man she met, the long distance relationship with a client that was so new the shine had not gone from it yet. Cady's situation, bringing up a

baby alone. And now this. The possibility that she might be another head strong career woman who had fallen at the womb hurdle. Her clock was not even ticking either, in fact, she wasn't even sure she had a clock. Magda sat and listened, refilling her coffee cup and nodding occasionally.
"So you think this man is nice man?"
George smiled. "Yes, yes I do. I have really fallen for him. It terrifies me, but it's true." He thought of the month she had just spent with him, and of her trip back to Paris that weekend, to finish the contract for two weeks.
Magda half smiled and then looked her straight in the eye.
"You want baby?"
George thought for a moment. Did she want a baby? The truth was, half of her did not look at the test in case it was negative, which was barmy but now, she really hoped she was.
"Yes, I want baby."
Magda grinned.
"We having baby then! I clean now yes, then we go to doctors. And shopping, oh the shopping. What fun we shall be having!"
She was up off her feet now, swilling out the cups and reaching for the hoover. George sat still at the table. Magda placed a ball of tissue in front of her and started singing as she went to hoover the lounge. George opened the ball to stare at the test. On the LCD screen one word was visible. PREGNANT. She couldn't wait to tell Ben.

***

Looking at the address in her hand a second time, she asked her driver "Is this really the right address?"
Simmons, her devoted and burly employee peered out of his window and said, "Afraid so, madam. Shall I drive you home?"
Priscilla nearly squealed "Yes Simmons, and don't spare the horse power," but instead she simply smoothed her hair, clutched her Radley bag to her and asked him to open the door.
Getting out, she surveyed the scene. The housing estate was glum to say the least. Most of the houses were quite neat, gardens fenced in and flowers blooming, but this small corner had a dark gloom about it. And she knew why. It was this house; it emanated a dark aura that seems to permeate through to the other houses. The fence was just a few sticks now, the rest knocked down. Broken plastic

toys in gaudy colours were strewn across the tufts of earth that passed for a lawn, the front window was broken and held together with masking tape, and the letter box was nailed shut. Everything was coated in a layer of grime and dirt, and there was a smell that Priscilla was sure would never come out of her Wool blend coat. Picking her steps, she gingerly walked to the front doorstep. Loud music blared out from the house, and she had to bang loudly for some time in the end, all the while casting nervous glances back at Simmons, who was now out of the car and stood by the open boot, probably with a tyre iron in his white gloved hands. Suddenly, the music stopped and shouting came from inside. The door banged open and a waft of fried food and cigarette smoke greeted her nostrils. Resisting the urge to pull out her smelling salts, she smiled at the woman before her. Tracey was clad in a tatty grey dressing gown that Priscilla guessed was once white, and had a small grubby looking infant, wrapped in a heaving nappy and day-glo pink t-shirt. Tracey's bottom lip was stuck out, a fag perched on it, and her scowl was made all the worse by the smoke that drifted up into her eyes.
"Yeah?" She looked at Priscilla in her finery, and eyed the driver with the flash motor behind.
"You the social? Don't look like it. Anyway, I told yer on the phone, cheque is in the post for the rent, and I 'aint paying the arrears off till I get a four bed. Little Tyrone and Brittany are cramped in that little box room, poor bleeders, and with one on the way…"
Priscilla's mouth dropped open.
"Er..actually Tracy, I'm Priscilla, Richard's mother. I have come to talk to you about Cady. She is in a bit of a mess…"
Tracy snorted loudly, switching the infant to her other hip and screaming behind her. "Lennox, turn that bleeding shite off! Cady, why, what's wrong with my little princess? Perfect life chaffing her perfect little arse is it?"
Priscilla continued over the din of the house.
"No, but with the baby coming and Richard passing, I.. I thought…"
She realised what a mistake she had made. No wonder Cady never spoke of her parents. Her mother obviously did not care about her daughter's wellbeing at all.

Tracy was eying her now, and shoving the infant into the arms of a man stood behind her in nothing but a pair of grey boxers, she smiled slowly, showing yellow teeth.
"Richard died, did he? And Cady's having a bairn? Why didn't you say so love? I'll get me coat."
As Priscilla bundled Tracy and her 3 kids into the car much to Simmons' bemusement, Richard looked down at the strange tableau before him and suddenly felt so angry. He never realised that Cady's mum was like this. To be fair, he had never met her parents, or even knew she had siblings. Did Cady even know? She felt sure that Cady would not ignore brothers or sisters should she have known. What a shmuck he was. No wonder Cady wanted a family of her own, a nice home. She never did anything wrong, really. She just turned from an independent party girl to a devoted housewife, which was just what he wanted really. And while she had allowed her light to be dimmed slightly day by day, year by year, he had taken the limelight and done just what he wanted, including sleeping with whomever he wanted. And now his mother, albeit with pure intentions, had released this woman on Cady. And Richard had a feeling it would not end well. Turning to Gerty, he pointed at the car.
"Can I use my rage now? I don't want that woman near my family, if Cady doesn't want it."
Gerty smiled and walked over to him.
"Let's see what we can do, eh child?"
Pulling up at Cady's house two hours later, stressed, tired, hungry and dishevelled, Priscilla and her entourage were just glad to get there. It was dusk now, and the wind picked up suddenly, sweeping the rubbish and leaves from the pavement straight into their dirty faces. Having had car trouble, with Simmons' and the AA man bemused whilst tinkering under the hood, Priscilla had been left to talk to Tracy, while she moaned about her piles, back ache and peppering her with questions about Cady. Strangely, she never asked how Richard died, or how Cady was, or the baby, she seemed more interested on what Cady would do about work and the house now she was a widow. Priscilla realised that she had made a big mistake. She had been trying to help, I mean, everyone needs their mum in situations like this, right?

Looking at the house bathed in light from the downstairs windows, with the neat front path and fragrant window boxes, she realised that Cady was doing ok, and she would be a better mother than she had perhaps had as an example.
Priscilla sighed and walked to the door.

Cady heard her mother before she saw her. With one ear to the door as she made a spaghetti bolognaise, she could pick out her mum's screechy tones before the doorbell went. Turning down the CD that was playing Nina Simone in the background, she considered turning off the lights and pretending that she wasn't in, but with Marcus due to arrive to help her clear out the study, she couldn't risk them meeting at the door.
She straightened her white blouse over her black skinny jeans, and glimpsing her pale panicked expression in the hall mirror and pulling a face at her own reflection, she opened the door.
"Hello mother. To what do I owe this....Priscilla?"
The sight of her mother-in-law looking dirty and guilty behind Tracy was the biggest shock of all. "What..why?"
Priscilla stepped forward, taking Cady's arm and leading her to the lounge like one would a confused old lady. "I went to see your mother today, I thought that you might need some family around you at a time like this, and she…well she is here now. Is something burning?"
Cady dashed to the stove, taking the food off the heat. Banging the oven door open, she shoved some cheese and garlic topped bruschetta slices under the grill and glared at the pair.
"I am fine, Priscilla. I don't need any help. I am cooking, I cleaned today. I am fine, see?" She gestured to the very homely looking sitting room. Priscilla nodded feebly and sank into the nearest armchair.
For the whole exchange Cady could see Tracy walking around the room, eyeing her knick knacks. Picking up the CD, she snorted loudly.
"Nina Simon? Who's that like, bit old in'it?"
Cady took the CD case back from her mother and placed it back on the rack.
"It's Nina Simone, mother, and I like it. Now what are you doing here? Kids ok?"

Tracy narrowed her eyes. “Always, and another on the way too. Some of us women find it easy that way.” She said this with a great degree of smugness, rubbing her stomach with her nicotine stained fingers.
Cady’s mouth dropped with shock, and she suddenly looked quite sick.
“Another? Who to this time, or don’t you know?”
Tracy’s grin froze on her lips. “It’s Wayne’s again, actually, and we are chuffed to bits.”
Cady walked back to the kitchen area and checking on her food, her eyes flicked to the kitchen clock. Marcus would be here any minute.
“Well ladies, not to be rude, but I am rather busy this evening, so is that all?”
She locked eyes with her mother as she said this, crossing her arms in obvious anger.
Priscilla watched the two pregnant women, so different, but with so much in common, circle each other like lionesses, complete with claws and raised hairs. She swore she heard Tracy growl at one point.
“Way I see it, dear daughter, is that you will have a pretty nice set-up here now, and with a little brother or sister on the way…I want more money.”
Priscilla’s eyes widened. *More money?*
Cady sighed loudly, and putting her shaking hands down by her sides, making fists so clenched they become almost completely white, she began walking across the carpet to her mother, her bare feet padding against the pile.
“What you are growing is NOT a brother or sister to me, or a child to be loved for you. It’s a meal ticket, like we all were. Now I have done my bit with the monthly cheque, but I am not returning to work for a while, so money will be tight. You have had more than your pound of flesh, and I think it’s time for me to cut my losses.”
Tracy exploded. “Cut your losses! You ungrateful bitch! You think you’re so fucking hoity toity don’t you!? You really think this life is yours? Cos it’s not love, you are alone now, and pretty soon you will be at the housing office pleading your belly like the rest of us. You think she,” pointing a yellow finger at Priscilla,” will look

after ya? You are kidding yourself love. You are not stopping giving me my due either, girl."
At this the lights flickered on and off. The CD burst into life, playing Nina's 'Ain't Got No.' Tracy jumped and the three women all looked wide eyed at each other. Priscilla seemed calmer somehow, she stayed in her seat, pulling a cushion to her chest tightly as though she were about to visit a movie. The words played out, *'ain't got no home, ain't got no shoes, ain't got no money, ain't got no class'* as the cushions from the sofa started to pelt at Tracy, knocking her back towards the door.

Cady was terrified. What the hell was happening? The CD kept singing the same lines over and over, while the cushions were attacking Tracy like stuffed ninjas. Tracy was stumbling backwards to the door, screaming obscenities all the way at Cady. The lights were flickering on and off frantically, and the whole room jiggled and clanged around as though they were on board a train. Cady turned to Priscilla and stopped dead. Priscilla was staring at the ceiling, smiling the warmest smile that Cady had ever seen. Then she realised she had seen it before. When she had looked at her son. A look of complete admiration and adoration. *This was Richard? No, that was crazy!*
Tracy continued to scream and the front door suddenly flung itself open. Cady ran towards her mother as the wind whipped around the door step. Tracy's greasy hair was flapping in tendrils about her face, and she was screaming now as the wind whipped her about. Expecting a worried Marcus at the door having heard the commotion, she realised that there was no-one there. She jumped back from the door as realisation set in. *Richard was helping her. It had to be him. Either that or she was having a stroke. Either way, it gave her the push she needed.*
Shouting against the now howling wind and grabbing at her own hair as it consumed the features of her face, she yelled, "Mum, I never want to see you again, and you will never get another penny. YOU ARE ON YOUR OWN!"
It all stopped. The cushions dropped to the floor, the wind died, the CD stopped and the lights came back on. Looking behind her, Cady could see her lounge was intact, if a little windswept, and

Priscilla was still sitting in the chair. Giving her two thumbs up, she turned to the ceiling and blew a kiss.
Cady looked at her mum, snarling and sweating on her doorstep and smiled.
"Goodbye mother."
And with that she slammed the door tight.

CHAPTER 20

A MONTH LATER

Cady awoke to the sunlight streaming through her window and smiled before she even realised it. She felt at peace for a change, which was an achievement judging by what the last few months had entailed. The door went downstairs, heralding Luke's arrival for work; He had his own key and often came and went as he pleased. Shame he was involved, she thought to herself, before pushing the thought away. From the hushed phone calls and the odd arguments she had picked up on, he was obviously in some kind of relationship, and since she was a pregnant widow, what right did she have to pry?
She shrugged to herself and hauling her ever expanding body out of the spare room, threw on a dressing gown over her maternity nightshirt which read 'Bump 'n' Grind' and went downstairs to greet him. But it wasn't Luke who stood at the bottom of the stairs to greet her. It was a woman. A woman dressed up to the nines in a leather skirt and miniscule t-shirt adorned with the word 'bitch' stood before her, glaring straight at her.
"Er, can I help you?" Cady asked, shocked at the fact that this strange woman had walked straight into her house. A sudden errant thought made her shudder. *Was this the other woman?*
"Yes, you can help me, you can stop taking up Luke's time on this job, he's here all hours, late nights…Luke has a life too, you know. You have to stop being a slave driver. We don't all live off our rich husbands in la-la ladies that lunch land, you understand?"
The woman put her hands on her tiny hips and pouted at her, obviously challenging her to answer. Cady was aghast. At first she was relieved that it wasn't Richard's floozy, but she had an uneasy feeling in the pit of her stomach now when she thought of Luke with this woman. What was wrong with her?
More to the point, *what had Luke been telling this girl?*
She thought of him, laughing with this woman while they frolicked about, semi-naked, drinking champagne, laughing at the poor

knocked up posh princess. She mentally shook herself. Everything she had learned about Luke told her that he was a good man, the opposite to this woman, and why had she pictured them half nude? It so must be the pregnancy hormones….after all, she was with Marcus, wasn't she?
The woman started tapping her heel on the wood hall floor and Cady realised that her inner monologue had been playing out on her face while the woman stood waiting for an answer. Clearing her throat, Cady placed her hand absentmindedly on her bump and looked the woman square in the eye, trying her best to look as calm and nonchalant as possible, not an easy feat in her condition.
"Look, Luke WORKS for me, as my employee. I am in a relationship, and as you can plainly see, I am in no state for sexual escapades, with Luke or anyone else for that matter. I am not up to this, so I suggest that you talk to Luke, and LEAVE. NOW."

Victoria pushed out her small perky boobs and made for the door. Just as she was leaving through the open door, she called out, "He is mine you know, he just needs reminding how much he loves me. I don't see you as a threat anymore." Looking her up and down again, she snorted derisively and clicked clacked down the steps. Cady sat down on the stairs, or rather reversed slowly onto it. She had let the woman rattle her; that was for sure. Why she was bothered, she had no idea. After all, why should she care what Luke did? She was with Marcus, and her baby was due in two months, she had so much to do, she had no time to think about Luke. Shaking her head, she went upstairs. Now the study was cleared of paperwork and books, she was going to claim the space for herself. She had always fancied writing children's books, she was quite good at writing stories as a child, and she had nothing but time to fill now she had handed in her notice at the law firm, so why not. Maybe she would even take a few courses. Noting the empty bookshelves, save for a few of her own paperbacks, and the huge imposing oak desk, she closed the door. Time to go shopping, Cady, shopping for your new life. She needed to make a start on the baby things too, she had not ventured to the shops other than the supermarket and Mothercare for a few maternity clothes, and time was getting on now. The books all spoke of equipment, essentials and hospital bag must haves, and so far all she had dug out was her old dusty gym holdall. She really did need to open the letter from Richard too and turn on her mobile, that would take her mind of…*mind off what, Luke?* What the hell was going on! Hearing Luke come in and shout up hello to her, she raced off to the spare room to get ready. The master bedroom was another thing to go on the list she realised. She would fill that list so full that she had no time to think till the baby arrived, and then everything would be fine. She just knew it would. Luke would be finished on the project, the bubs would be here, and she could start her new life. And maybe Marcus could be part of it too, at some point. She had kept him at arms length so far, so other than a few lunches and walks in the park, they had not seen each other, and she had tried to keep Luke and Marcus apart. Not for any reason of course, there was just no reason for the two worlds to collide. Dressing in her nicest maternity dress, she pulled on her jacket and slinky (but flat heeled) boots and sauntered down the stairs to go shopping. And buy a notepad for that to-do list.

CHAPTER 21

Magda squealed at the window display. "Georgina, you hev to look at this! How tiny cute are these, eh?" She gesticulated wildly at the display of yellow and orange jumpsuits, draped across various cuddly giraffes in the shop window. George nodded and smiled briefly, before burying her head back in her Blackberry.
"Miss, no work today, ok? You hev to start buying for baby, little one be here in de spring, that is not long now. Be here before you know it, little baby shooting out your er, vag, you call, yes?"
George lowered the phone and raised her eyebrows. "Magda! Sshhh!"
She giggled at her maid despite herself. Magda had become a great friend to her recently, and she DID need to start getting ready for the baby. She had been trying Ben for a few days now though, and his phone was constantly off. They had not spoken much since her last France trip, and anxieties were starting to creep in, despite her hard shell. Ben had been pleased about the baby, and had promised to come over to the UK that weekend to form a plan for how the whole thing would work, where they would live etc. The contact since her return however had trailed off somewhat, Ben always complaining of being tired or busy, and their daily chats and texts had dropped to the odd e-mail, and now nothing.
She shrugged off the uneasy feeling in her stomach and smiling at Magda, they walked into the boutique and set to work. Twenty minutes later, they had bought half of the shop, burned some plastic and George felt better. She actually felt quite content and mumsy, which was not entirely as horrifying as she imagined. Laughing with Magda as the assistant started to box up their epic pile of purchases, her phone rang. Thinking it was Ben due to the Paris number, she answered.
"Oh hi darling, you won't believe where I am…"
"Miss Elliott, it's Ed Marshall here, from Marshall and Marshall. I am calling to tell you that your services will no longer be required on the contract any further, and we shall send your final payment today by bank transfer as before. And thanks very much for a job well done."

George's throat went dry, and she leaned on the counter for support.
"Er, thank you, that's er,…is Ben, Mr Williamson available?"
Ed paused. "Miss Elliott, as I said, your services are no longer required. These instructions have come from Mr Williamson himself. He asked me to call you."
George swallowed hard. "I understand, ah, thanks."
Hearing the line click, she put her phone back in her bag. Magda was busy chatting with the shop assistant, both of them cooing over the little bundles of clothes and other baby paraphernalia. George's ears buzzed and her head swam. Turning to look at the window, the display of jaunty giraffes caught her eye. Walking to the display, she pulled herself up into the window and grabbed one of the giraffes. That was when she lost it. Pulling the head off the stuffed toy, she threw it behind her and moved onto the next. She howled as though in pain as she proceeded to decapitate the toys one by one, screaming and crying as she went. Magda and Helen the shop owner stared in horror as the immaculately dressed pregnant woman proceeded to destroy the display piece by piece. Jumping down from the window, she sank to the floor and burst into racking sobs. Helen went to make a cup of tea for them all. With the amount that was available on her credit card, she was not worried about her stock, she was more concerned with looking after her now best customer. People have strange priorities in a recession. Magda sat by George and held her tight. No words were needed.
The tinkle of the shop door heralded the arrival of a new customer, and George was suddenly self conscious. Looking up at the arrival, she looked straight at a very pregnant, and very surprised Cady. Taking in the surroundings around her, she stooped with difficulty to pick up the discarded head of a toy monkey.
George started to cry anew at the sight of her friend.
Cady smiled. "Hungry girls? I am starving, fancy some lunch?"

***

An hour later, all three women were sat in Cady's sitting room, takeaway coffees, sandwiches and buns spread out on the coffee

table. Even noises from the builders in the background did not dull their conversation.
"So you have not heard from her since?"
Cady shook her head. "No, and I stopped the standing order from my bank, so she will get no more money, and she hasn't even phoned to give me an ear bashing! It's strange, but I feel relieved." She smiled, grabbing another cheese and pickle sandwich happily. Georgina looked at Cady, and winced at the words she was about to speak.
"So, you really think it was Richard that 'came'? Were you not scared?"
"I was petrified at first, but Priscilla was here and she seemed happy about it, and then I just felt strength, like I had an unseen ally, so I told her where to go, which I have never dared do before. I know I should be freaked out, but I'm not. I am still furious with him, but I am glad that he is alright, in a way."
George's eyebrows raised.
"You know what I mean, he is dead, obviously, but the fact he came to help me, that means he is okay and it's kinda nice to think he knows that he is a father."
Magda picked up a Viennese finger and licked some of the cream from the side.
"Is kinda nice, yes? That he say sorry, before he go. I think it quite the romance gesture. Back from ze dead to stick up against the mother-in-law. Very Nicholas Sparksie, no?" She shoved the rest of the sweet treat in her mouth.
Cady and George burst into laughter, and then stopped when they eyed each other.
"What are you going to do, George? Will you be keeping the baby?" Cady said softly, not wanting to jeopardise their newly rekindled friendship. Georgina smoothed down her clothes self-consciously, her brows furrowed in thought.
"I am going to keep it Cades, I know what I said, and I am so sorry for that, but I..I have changed, I guess, or rather the baby has changed me. I am actually quite excited, and Magda will help me when I go back to work." Magda nodded at this, still chewing. "I am planning to tell my boss tomorrow actually, I am going in and clearing my desk for a week off, and I am going to tell him that I am office bound from now on, no more travelling around." George

looked rosy cheeked at the very prospect of telling her boss her demands.
"But what if he doesn't agree?" Cady asked, picking up another sandwich. Man she was hungry today.
"I will tell him I quit then, I still have all that money saved from my parents, I figure I could go freelance, work from home or something, we will be okay. I think he will cave anyway, I bring too much business in for him to just throw me away."
Cady grinned. "You said 'we' – as in you and a BABY. Wow, George, I am so happy for you!"
She smiled back at her friend, and Magda piped up, "all happy but Ben. We get Ben good, he not happy much, when he see Magda all gun a blazing."
Cady was confused. "You're going to Paris? Really?"
George laughed. "Oh yes, tomorrow night after the office, Magda and I are flying to Paris, figured we would take a few days holiday there to rest before the baby comes, do a bit of clothes shopping and visit the beautiful bouncing dead-beat daddy."
Cady was aghast at her friend's resolve in the face of so many changes in her life. Looking around her half finished house and listening to the banging in the background, she realised that although she was changing the house, nothing had really been sorted out. She was going to be a single mother in just over a month, and the build was finished at the end of the week. She still had to empty the master and spare bedrooms ready for painting, the decorators had to come do the whole house, and she had to buy a whole nursery. Today's shopping trip, although great for her and George, had really been a damp squib in terms of baby shopping. And she still had that letter to open from Richard….she had learnt from Dick that she could afford to stay off for a long while with the money as long as she was careful, but she still couldn't bear to open that letter, scared of what personal thoughts might be written down on those pages. She looked again at her best friend, chatting away with Magda about their baby shopping trip in Paris, and she realised it was now or never. It was time to sort her life out once and for all, Luke and Marcus included.

CHAPTER 22

The day came when the build was due to end. Luke had been hovering around the site all day every day, only leaving when he had no excuse to stay. Cady took his phone buzzing to be the woman calling him home, and so tried not to mind when he went home, or notice his phone vibrations. The fact was, she couldn't stop thinking about Luke, her days were occupied with thoughts of him, the baby, Marcus, even Richard. She had spent the last few days cleaning out the remaining two rooms of Richard. The spare room was now empty and the furniture covered for painting. The master bedroom had been horrible to undertake; eventually she had just thrown the whole bed away, sheets and all, getting the workmen to lug the sofa bed from the spare room into there till her new king size bed could be delivered. She had given Priscilla first refusal on his clothes, but surprisingly his mother had simply said that she had come to terms with his passing and that his clothes should benefit others, so a very happy charity shop lady was soon in the possession of a good few bags of men's books, clothes and trinkets. Cady kept the photos and made a memory box for the baby, full of things of daddy; wedding photos, cufflinks, notes he had left to Cady in the early days. Now the house was done, all ready for the final painting next week, and then she could get to work on assembling the parts of her new life. Thank the Lord for online shopping, she had everything ready to be delivered in two weeks and Dick himself said that he and Priscilla would come and assemble the cot, hang pictures etc so that everything was in place. 4 weeks from now and she would be a mother, and the thought terrified her and delighted her in equal measure. She knew once the house was complete, then she could relax. She had even chosen a distance learning course with a university on writing children's books; she planned to study when the baby slept, ease herself into her new roles. She was even going to fill the baby's bookcase with children's books, great research for her and bonding time with the baby. She could finally see a happy ending of sorts in sight. If she didn't think of Marcus, that is..or Luke. Try as she might, she just couldn't see Marcus in her house feeding the baby, or snuggling against him in front of the TV. She realised that she felt no spark,

he had just been what he always was, a comfort and a friend. She just had to tell him.
Luke was a different matter. All week he looked as though he was trying to tell her something, and she had been deliberately avoiding him, sticking her head in the laptop or a catalogue whenever he roamed near. She knew what he was trying to tell her, that he realised she liked him but he was taken. That basically he saw her as a desperate woman, pregnant and alone, with no chance of tearing him away from his beloved girl, who was essentially a broom handle with boobs. She just couldn't bear to hear him say what she already picked up on, and she figured that after today, she wouldn't need to. So here she was, perched in hiding on her sofa bed, mobile phone and Richard's letter sat next to her. Fluffing the cushions up, she tried and failed to bring her knees nearer to her chest, man she was uncomfortable lately. This pregnancy lark was like trying to move about with a beach ball stuck up your top, but worse because a beach ball didn't give you heartburn at 3am, or jab you in the ribs with a swift right kick, or make you cry at the TV advert for pile cream.
Turning the phone on, she waited for the onslaught of messages. When the handset started to beep, she opened the back and ripped out the sim card. Any messages on there would only upset her, and what was the point in that? Putting in the new one she had ordered from the phone company, she scrolled down her list of contacts, firing off a text to Marcus. MARCUS, IT'S CADY. PLEASE COME TO MINE TONIGHT, ABOUT 7? WE NEED TO TALK. She hoped that he would not contact her beforehand, she really just wanted to clear the air and set him straight and then she could concentrate on the baby. Luke would be gone after today too..and that thought scared her more than anything, even facing labour alone. Priscilla had made noises about being at the birth, but she wasn't too keen on the idea of her mother-in-law staring at her business end, seeing her poo and so forth, and George was terrified about her own labour. Asking her to witness another beforehand was a bit much to ask even of a best friend. So she would do it alone, as she would motherhood. Her phone beeped back, jolting her from her thoughts.

WOW, BACK IN THE REAL WORLD EH GIRL? SORRY HUN, AM WORKING LATE, AND TOMORROW BUT CAN COME SAT AT 7? M XX
Cady was disappointed. Her final scan was the next morning, the doctor had ordered an extra one with her scare earlier on, and she really just wanted to clear her emotional decks before going there. Never mind though, work was work. She replied, OK, 7 SAT. C. She left off the kiss again, but he either had not picked up on the context of the texts or he was ignoring it as he didn't reply. Either way, it would all be over by Monday morning.
Putting the phone on the bed, she smiled at the photo on the screen. It was her and George on one of their wine nights in, both slightly sloshed and gurning for the camera. Hmm, most people had their husbands on their phones, or their kids, maybe that was a tell of hers she had only noticed now. Glancing at the envelope on the bed, she took a deep breath and pushing her thumb under the gummed flap, slowly ripped open the envelope. She pulled out the contents and let them fall onto the sheets. Richard's handwriting was visible across the folded pages, swirly and elegant, so unlike her own. He had always joked how she could have been a doctor with her illegible scrawl.

She unfolded the pages and smoothed out the crisp expensive vellum sheets. There were two documents, one stapled with the law firm letterhead on it. She knew it contained details of her settlement, so she pushed that aside and turned to the paper clipped handwritten letter. She rubbed her huge bump and was comforted when the bump kicked against her hand. *I'm here mum, read it...*

Dear Cady,
If you are reading this then no doubt I am gone. It's funny, working in the law you write wills and sign documents, never thinking much about the circumstances that make them come to pass, divorces, house sales, death. These things are all part and parcel of life, and the legal documents just make them civilised, but then I suppose life isn't civilised, is it?
This is something that I never understood and you always did. That life is for living, no matter what small thing or being makes it worth it.

Richard watched from above as she opened the letter, willing her to understand what he was trying to say in his repressed turn of phrase. He felt a lump in his throat the size of Brazil as he gazed at her sat reading, cradling her swollen belly as she teared up. “It’s so true what they say, you don’t know what you’ve got until it’s gone,” he said over his shoulder to Gerty, who touched his shoulder with her hand.
“I know, child, I know.”

The truth of it is, Cady, is that I never deserved you or even appreciated you while I was alive, and now that I am dead, I will no doubt have hurt you further by my passing. The only comfort I can retain is that you will be well looked after when I am gone.
I can only say how grateful I am for you, and I am sorry for my wrongdoings. I hope that you are happy, and have a good life.
Richard

Cady’s tears fell silently as she read the letter again. The wording was so Richard, all restrained and oddly formal, even in this letter of all things. Her mind briefly flashed to Luke, who in comparison was a fireball of childish energy, constantly sketching and jotting down ideas on note pads and even till receipts, so expressive and unrestrained.
Reading the last paragraph, she suddenly got a flash of Richard’s last words to her…

It was dark that night, a winter night when the sky was dipped in ink, even the stars were muted from their usual brilliance. It was cold outside, she remembered that the windows were all cloudy from the hot air inside battling it out with the cold air outside the sills of the house. She had cooked as usual after work, and was sat talking to George on the phone while waiting for Richard, her heel slipping off her foot as she sat on the stool sipping rose wine. Then Richard had banged in, calling her name. She ended her call and poured a glass for him. She still had it in her hand when he came bounding into the kitchen and blurted that he was leaving her for someone else, that she could keep the house, and that he was leaving that night. Cady didn’t even grasp her emotions when the wine was dripping off Richard’s nose onto his shirt. She remembered thinking, 'damn, why did I do that? I will have to wash it now so it doesn't stain.' Richard went upstairs, and by the time Cady had downed another drink and turned off the food, he was back, overnight bag in hand, ready to walk out of the door. When he got to the threshold, her brain whirred into gear and she chased him onto the front steps of the house. It had started to rain; the water was bounding down on them both accompanied with a deafening noise, and a flash of lightening highlighted her husband's features. They were screaming at each other, him telling her to calm down and stop making a show in front of the neighbours, her calling him all the names under the sun and some from under the earth as well. She was so furious, shocked and hurt she wanted to kill him then and there. When the first fork of lightning flashed she felt irritated that it had not jabbed him in his Armani clad arsehole.

Richard was shaking his head now, shouting to be heard over the thunder and the heavy rain. Droplets used his nose as a rain gutter, skiing off the end like lemmings.

"Cady, I'm sorry, I really am, but I have to leave. I want you to know, I wish you a very happy life. I am sure it will happen for you."

Cady was soaked to the skin, bare feet frozen to the stone steps of the house. Her white silk blouse was clinging to her frame like wet paper, and her hair hung in tendrils around her tortured features.

"You condescending bastard Richard!" She marched to the pavement edge to where he stood in the deserted road. "You fucking cheat on me again, leave me, and wish me a sodding happy life! Well you know what I wish Richard, I WISH YOU WOULD JUST DROP DEAD!"

It was then she heard the screech and watched her husband's face turn from anger, to shocked, to nothing. She heard a huge bang and scrunched up her eyes in surprise, feeling a warm splash of rain on her face. It was only when she opened her eyes that she saw that Richard wasn't there. He wasn't there, but a car was, there were people running towards it, shouting, screaming, and she didn't know why. Till she saw him: crumpled under the car, his briefcase on its side up the road, contents strewn everywhere. Pushing her hair away from her face and racing to fall beside him, she put out her hands to stroke his face as he looked at her, but her hands were not covered with warm rain. They were covered with blood, blood that looked like thick dark oil in the night's light. And Richard wasn't looking at her. He wasn't looking at anyone; he was gone.

***

Luke waved the builders off and went inside to straighten up. Looking around the house, he couldn't believe how big and open it was now. Once the painting was done and the furniture was arranged, he knew it would be fantastic. Just perfect for a little one too, and the whole house reeked of Cady now. Richard's pictures were all over the nursery, which was a nice touch, but the other rooms were all her now. Making two cups of tea, he went upstairs to find his client. He found her asleep on her side in the master bedroom, her face streaked with tears and a pile of papers clutched to her chest. Setting down the steaming mugs, he sat beside her and stroked the salty water away from her face. She roused and opened her blue eyes, looking straight at him. Before he could rationalise the thought away, he bent his head and kissed her gently on her closed lips. Confusion flashed across her face and then she opened her mouth slightly and kissed him back. He pulled her up and cradled her into his arms, legs smashed against each other on the bed, the papers cascading down his back as she put her arms around him. They explored each other's mouths; Luke felt a hot warm flash in his heart and his pulse raced. He loved this girl with all his heart, and now she was kissing him back, running his hair through her fingers. They kept kissing and hugging each other tight till Luke's phone rang. He groaned and they both laughed, Luke not letting go of her while he reached his phone out of his pocket. The moment was broken when she saw his face. A look of discomfort flashed across it; she knew it was the woman. She pulled away from him and straightened herself up, as much as a horny pregnant woman could in this situation.
Luke thrust the phone back into his pocket and reached for her. She stilled his hand and cleared her throat.
"I wanted to talk to you actually Luke, to say thank you for everything, I am really grateful but obviously now the house is finished..so.."

Luke broke in. “So, you need a hand when the paint’s dry? That’s good, because I was thinking, I could take you to the scan in the morning, Dad will lend me his car, and then I thought that we could hit the sculpture park with a picnic, I have something to show you. When the workers are done, I can help you finish the house off and then..”
“Luke,” she half screamed, half spat, “the job is over now. I am grateful, but you have your own life to lead, and your girlf..”
Luke rolled his eyes. “Ooh, I get it! No, Cady, no, that woman who keeps phoning is an ex, an unwanted ex. I am not seeing anyone, Cades, and the fact is that I want to see you, don’t you get that?”
Cady shook her head, remembering how adamant the woman was about her and Luke reconciling, she couldn’t risk her heart like that, even for him. “Luke, don’t say anymore please. Just go back to your life.”
Luke opened his mouth to speak, but she cut him off.
“Luke, I am serious. I am with Marcus and I am happy. I’m sorry about the kiss, it was just the hormones.”
She kept her eyes focused on the pattern on the quilt, not daring to look at him in case she threw her wrestler weight body against him and begged him to stay, to choose her forever. She just couldn’t be second best again, and she had vowed that her baby would never feel that pain either.
Luke swallowed hard, gave her a lingering peck on the lips, and was gone. When she heard the door bang shut, she rolled herself under the quilt and fell straight to sleep, heart aching with every strained beat.

***

Luke was at his apartment door before he even realised he had left Cady’s doorstep. His mind was a swirl of emotions, most of those emotions involving striding up to that posh twat Marcus and punching him in his smug, moisturised face.
He just didn’t like the guy, and if they were seeing each other, where was he? He never came to the house and Luke had never heard Cady talk on the phone with him. In fact during their time together she never mentioned Marcus at all. What kind of name

was Marcus anyway? Luke snorted to himself, turning the key to his home.
He was just taking advantage of Cady, hopefully she was see that before he had a chance to bond with the baby. When Luke thought of the baby a warm feeling spread throughout his body, he couldn't wait to meet the little person who had already made a dent on his heart, and he hoped he would at least get to do that once. It seemed that once the baby was born, they would become a little family, and that left Luke right where he started, except he felt like a completely different person than he did a few short months ago.
Dumping his rucksack down on the hook by the door, he walked through to the open plan kitchen, clicking the answering machine and coffee machine buttons as he went.
As the aroma of rich roasted filled the apartment, which was a welcome change from the smell of paint and canvases, he thumbed through his post, listening as the gallery's administrator gave him the final details for the exhibition. The Hepworth was showing his work that very weekend, and this was Luke's big break. He had been working for months in his spare time, which had been even harder since he couldn't seem to tear himself away from Cady at all.
The second message jolted his mind back to the machine as Vicky's nasally whining tones came across the answering machine.
"Lukey baby, you haven't been answering my calls, I hope you are not angry that I spoke to your client, but she needed to know where she stood. Call me, we need to talk."
Luke face palmed and groaned loudly. Jesus Christ, no wonder Cady acted like she did! He decided to go round the following day, and drag her along to the gallery showing if he had to. Once she was there, he felt sure he could make her understand. Then he remembered Marcus and his heart sank. They would be going to the scan together, and then probably spending the weekend together, polishing his Mercedes or going to the Oprah, if Marcus chose. He just couldn't see Cady with him anymore then he could believe she was married to Richard. The pictures he had seen of him made him think that he was a bit posh too, a bit stuffy. Cady was the opposite, she just needed to realise it for herself. Sighing, he poured a big cup of coffee and sat down before the canvas in front of his stool. Staring at the white screen, he realised that he

wouldn't talk to Cady, he would leave her. She had made her choice, Marcus was like Richard and maybe that WAS what she wanted, and he could never compete with the salary, not till the commissions started coming in, if they ever did.
He took a huge glug of the strong brew and reached for his brush. He had one more piece to finish for the showing. The brush however, had other ideas. As his fingers reached for the handle, it quivered. Jumped twice, quivered again, and then dipped itself into the blue paint. Luke stared at the blue paint pot in horror. He sniffed his coffee and went to pour it down the drain. *Great,* he thought, *caffeine, heartbreak and no sleep add up to a crazy artiste.* He refilled his cup and taking a hesitant breath, reached out a shaking hand towards the brush. It jumped again. He grabbed the brush and squeaked out a yelp as it headed for the canvas, taking his arm with it.
"What! Ahh!"
The brush swirled and looped. Luke could only stare at his own hand being moved by unseen forces, blue paint flecks flicking off in all directions with the urgency of the movements. His hand stopped and the brush fell to the floor. Snatching his hand back, he stared at the pattern the paint had made.
Fight for her.
"What?" Luke's eyes bulged. His spine was ice cold and he felt hot and sick. His ears were ringing in his head. Looking at the ceiling of his apartment, he softly asked, "For Cady?"
The brush jumped up from the floor, swirling on the canvas once more.
Yes, fight for her. Fight for them both.
Luke struggled to get breath even to speak.
"Richard?"
YES! Fight for her, NOW.
The brush dropped to the floor, splattering paint on his black jeans. He jumped as a bang resounded behind him. His rucksack had dropped, or been pulled off the hook, his gallery flyers were scattered across the floor.
Luke ran both hands through his hair.
"Ok Richard, I get it."
He smiled at the ceiling. He was either crazy, or the dead husband of the woman he loved had just given him a kick up the backside.

CHAPTER 23

Georgina squinted against the Parisian sun and stuffed another pain au chocolat into her slightly expanding face. The last few days in France had been amazing; Magda was a brilliant friend now rather than an employee, and she was so excited about that baby that George had been swept up by the excitement too, and now she couldn't wait till the baby came in March. She had visions of her and Cady round the Christmas table with Magda, pulling crackers, George with her bump and Cady with her little baby. She had never really had a family scene like that before, unorthodox as it was, and she felt…content. Work seemed like a million miles away, and for once, she was glad about that. Her boss had caved to her demands and practically kissed her feet with relief that she wasn't leaving altogether. He had agreed that she could work from home and come to meetings a couple of times a month, and had worked with her on the no more travel clause too. George felt that she could probably travel a little for work, once she was in a routine. Magda would come too, and they could make a holiday out of it. It would be lovely for her baby to be a globe trotter, and a welcome change from her previous life in hotels. She realised now how lonely she had felt, but now she had a new life to worry about, and she was going to do the best for her child, no matter what.

She had e-mailed her parents to tell them about the baby, she contained no details about the father, just that she was happy and would continue to work. She had her response two days later, when a delivery man from Kiddicare showed up with the deluxe baby shower package, complete with stuffed toys and breast pump. The note said, "Plane tickets here when you want them darling, get Junior a passport. Much love, Mummy and Daddy."
Magda was incensed and swore in her native tongue for a few days every time she passed the huge basket, which took up half of the newly decorated nursery. George however, felt it was a huge step for her parents to want her to visit, and she kept the note in her bedside table, the first scrap of her parents she had kept for years.

The next day, she went to the post office and got a passport application form, placing the paperwork next to the note.
Becoming aware that Magda was staring at her, she reached for her tea cup and brushed the pastry crumbs from her lips.
"You is so happy, Georgina, it pleases me so. Why you want do this? Only upset yourself, seeing that pig again."
Magda turned her head to the right, spitting onto the pavement at the word pig, making a French man wobble on his bike as he passed. The street café was a block from Ben's office, and as today was the self imposed deadline that George had set herself, they were sat outside fuelling up before battle. Magda had called the office that morning pretending to be a prospective client and ascertained that Ben would be in the office all afternoon. They had a fake appointment at 2pm, and it was 1.35pm now.
Finishing up their lunch, they walked in silence to the offices of Marshall & Marshall. Magda kept casting furtive side glances at her pregnant friend, worried about the toll this encounter would take on her. She, like Cady, realised that for all her independence and inner fire, George was really a frightened girl underneath, never having quite got over the abandonment of her parents. And here she was, fighting for a father for her unborn child, who had been cast aside before even meeting each other.
She reached out to grab the door for her, as a man on the other side pushed his way through. They both started to apologise to each other, till Magda caught George's shocked expression and stopped talking. The man, immaculately dressed in a smart suit, was arm in arm with a very slim, very stylish dark haired woman. Ben's own face dropped to the floor when he saw her standing there, and before they could react, he simply steered the woman hurriedly into a waiting limo, and they were gone. George felt the woman's eyes appraise her momentarily before dismissing her as no threat.
Magda just managed to catch George as she fainted and hit the floor.
Four hours later, they were sat on a plane for home, George staring into space as she rubbed her slightly rounded belly.
All she could murmur was, "He would have missed our appointment. Not very professional."
Magda nodded. She had raced into the offices to fetch help, and as the security guard was tending to George, she had left a note for

the delightful Ben informing him of their intentions that day. She made a mental note to learn to write swear words in English, as she felt sure he would not get the full tone of her letter. She could only hope he knew some Hungarian. She wanted him to feel George's pain, and her wrath. Stupid pig headed men, never knew what they had. She had come here to follow a man, a promise of a new life. Well she had a new life, and she was proud of that, but she was a fighter without a baby in tow. Magda decided there and then that she would help George in any way she could, starting with taking a night course in childcare, so that she could look after the baby the best she could and make the little one so happy and content that it would never feel the loss of losing a parent before their own birth. Magda surmised that Cady was in the same boat, the babies would be close in age, so they would all grow up together, women and babies.

***

Cady frowned as she saw her empty mobile screen. No messages from Magda or George, and that could only mean bad news, since it was D-Day for Ben. She shifted her weight in the uncomfortable plastic chair she was sat in. She didn't see the point of a scan this late on, she was due any day and the baby was fine kicking away, as much as it could in the confines of her now cramped womb. The doctor was an old friend of Dick's, and the anxious grandparents had insisted on the extra check ups, and paying the bill themselves. Cady had gone along with it for a quiet life, the baby was as precious to them as it was her, after all and their concern was a stark contrast from her own upbringing. She was glad that the baby would have them in its life. She was adamant on one thing though, the sex of the baby would be a surprise, and Priscilla had reluctantly agreed, muttering to herself about Tiffany rattles and matching ribbons.

It was a warm day for September, and even the air conditioning in the private clinic felt like something blowing pathetically from the other side of the room. She shuffled her sandaled feet on the floor and checking no-one was looking, adjusted her huge kidney warming pants under her yellow sun dress. She had felt so great

that morning, not too tired or bulky, but when she looked in the mirror, all she saw was a huge overweight canary with cankles. Still, she had no-one to dress up for, and when the baby came, she would be lucky to brush her hair, let alone put some slap on. Technically of course, she reminded herself, she still had a boyfriend of sorts, but tonight that would all change. She just hoped that Marcus would be okay with her decision. The last thing she wanted was to hurt him.
Looking around the pristine empty waiting room for the fiftieth time, she spied a neat stack of high end magazines, and she was just starting to manoeuvre herself from the chair when the door to the doctor's office opened. Out came Angela from the office, immaculate as always in a beautiful flowing kaftan and skyscraper heels. Cady double blinked as Angela turned to her side, still engrossed with the doctor. She was pregnant! Quite heavily so too, she couldn't quite believe it! She was still processing the event when Marcus strode out of the doctor's office behind her, stopping right in front of Cady. His face turned drip white, and his mouth opened and closed like a fish gasping for air. Cady was frozen in place, arms lifting her half off the chair, and she started to wobble. Marcus was at her side in an instant, lowering her back onto the chair. Cady ignored the sticking of her thighs to the hard plastic as she looked dumbfounded into Marcus's eyes. He just stared back, a look of guilt and sorrow plastered across his face from his contorted mouth to his crinkled eyes.

Angela turned from the doctor now, a smug look on her face. "Oh hello Cady, darling, oh wow, are you still pregnant? You look positively fed up! Marcus darling, be a dear and bring the car around please, I am ever so tired this morning."
Cady couldn't compute what she was seeing. Her cheeks flushed red and she felt the prick of hot tears in her eyes, threatening to give her away. She had decided that she and Marcus weren't right, sure, but that was a moot point now, and Cady was yet again the unwilling other woman. She wrapped her arms around her bump protectively and smiled weakly at Angela.
Marcus found his voice and flashing a dirty look at Angela, which she smirked at, he turned back to Cady, kneeling at her feet.

"Cady, It was a one off, the night of the funeral. I'm sorry, I was so-"
"Darling, NOW please, we do have a lot to do this weekend if we are going to finish the nursery, Daddy." Angela tapped her heel sharply, giggling nervously at the doctor.

Her barb hit Cady like a hail of gunfire. She flinched and shaking her head, looked down at her feet. She wanted to curl up and cry. Marcus started towards the door reluctantly, turning to her on his way out saying, "Angela, you really are a bitch sometimes." Cady could feel the waves of anger emanating from him.
Angela's tinkling laughter rang out in the high ceilinged room. The doctor, looking a little dumbfounded at this display, drew a scan photo from his file.
"So, you are right on schedule for your 39 week caesarean, so I shall see you in October." Angela grabbed at the scan picture and thrust it into her bag, cutting the doctor off before he could finish. Cady's head snapped up. October? Richard wasn't even dead when she conceived! What? Cady felt sick as realisation set in, and one look at Angela's guilty face confirmed what she suspected. Angela was the woman that Richard was leaving her for, and that was Richard's baby. Poor Marcus, she thought as she leant forward and vomited all over Angela's pristine heels. *Two for two, she thought numbly as she heard Angela shriek.* The doctor sighed and called for the nurse.

Watching from above, Gerty shook her head and looked at Richard, who was sat on the floor, head in hands.
"Not to kick a fellow soul when he's down, but did you never hear of contraception? That's two babies, two baby mamas, no daddy? That's not a nice legacy to leave behind, child."
Richard nodded. "I know that, Gerty! I never knew when I was alive though did I! Angela is trying to palm my child off on my best friend, who really wants my wife! It's like a sitcom, I couldn't make it up if I tried! What can I do though?"
Gerty nodded back to the scene before them. "Concentrate on those two, the family that could be. The other child will be fine, honey. Angela will look after it, I'm sure."

Richard looked back at the hospital to see Luke pull up outside. He was just about to go through the doors when he spied Marcus waiting outside. Shaking his head, Luke turned and rode away again on his bike.
"*He thinks they are together, you need to sort that out, and free that man from his prison.*"
Richard nodded. "Cady will sort this out, if any one can, she can. I just have to show her the way. Can you help me?
Gerty furtively looked around the expansive white room. She sat next to Richard and bent close to his ear.
"We can, but it will be hard, it will take a lot out of you, and you will need to harness your anger into what you need. You ready?"
Richard had never felt so ready in his afterlife. "I am ready, I need to right my wrongs."

CHAPTER 24

Georgina unpacked the last of the Parisian baby shopping in the now completed nursery. She knew she had worried Magda, but she felt so hurt that she couldn't trust herself to talk to anyone about it without bursting into tears. She felt the rejection on a whole new level, her parents leaving for the States was a walk in the park compared to the punch she had felt in her heart seeing Ben and that woman in France. He looked so shocked and terrified at her presence, it had brought her to the realisation that he was embarrassed, ashamed of her even. He had not just rejected her, but their child too, and the thought of relating that tale to her child one day was heartbreaking. She shuddered to even think about it; she knew exactly how her child would feel, because she had gone through it herself. She didn't like to think what was worse, having the parents in your life then abandoning you, or knowing that they never wanted you at all. Looking around the room at all the beautiful things, she felt a fluttering in her tummy. Only a slight fluttering, and it could well have been the huge fruit salad she had devoured earlier, but she felt sure it was the baby, giving her a sign. A thank you, recognition that her mother had tried and that they would be okay. George rubbed her bump and shouted to Magda, "Hey Mags, you fancy a movie tonight?"
They would be just fine, stuff Ben. Independence all the way from now on. At least the baby would be a fluent speaker of Hungarian cuss words, not many parents could say that about their child.

***

Cady was in the kitchen giving her already immaculate worktops another scrub. Her whole house was finished, painted and cleaned from top to bottom. Her bag was packed for the hospital and there was a stack of brand new unread books in the living room to keep her occupied. She had enrolled on her Children's Writing course, and was due to start in four months time on distance learning. She was ready, and she was bored. Marcus kept popping to the forefront of her mind, him and that scavenging bitch Angela. Two men in Cady's life and Angela had stolen them both. Not only that, but she was planning on bringing Richard's baby up with Marcus, a plan that Cady herself had considered in her early days of confusion and grief. She didn't know what to do for the best. Putting away her cloth, she made a cup of tea and sat down on her new couch. She was just thumbing through the pile of paperbacks when one of them fell to the floor, a pen on the table rolling after it. She started to bend down, and gasped as she saw the book flip open and the inside cover starting to fill with writing from the pen. A pen that was moving by itself in a hurried fashion, producing Richard's handwriting.

Tell Marcus the truth..

Cady put her hands to her face, knowing that he had been there that morning. It was an eerie but comforting feeling, knowing for sure that he knew about his babies. She nodded, "I will Richard, I'm sorry for what she did. Even you didn't deserve that."

The pen continued to write faster and faster.

Gallery...Luke...make it right..go to him now.

Cady frowned. "Richard, as weird as this is, you setting me up on dates from beyond the grave, Luke's got-"

The pen bounced twice, stabbing the paper hard with its black nib. It wrote again, swirling and looping, the pages turning and turning as he filled them with scrawl.

"Okay okay!" Cady grabbed the book, scared now by the frantic movements.

Flipping the pages, it said the same all over,

Tell Marcus the truth. Go to the Gallery now..find Luke..be happy.

Cady sat back on the couch, clutching the book. Reaching for the phone, she dialled a number.

"Taxi? Gallery please, and make it fast."

She hugged the book and setting it down, waddled for her shoes and coat.

"Wish me luck Richard."

From above, a drained Richard smiled weakly. "Go get him, Cady."

The Gallery was lit up from the inside as Cady walked across the white walkway to the front doors. The river raged underneath and

she felt a little dizzy, grabbing the bars momentarily as she steadied her wide gait.
Reaching the reception area, she looked for him in the café, but he was nowhere to be found. Coming back to the foyer, she spied a large display on an easel.
Starting tonight, Luke Masters Exhibition, Gallery One

She blinked at his name. He had been trying to tell her about this the other day, and she had never let him speak. Cursing herself for listening to the Vile Victoria, she started up the stairs to the gallery.
It was all huge white rooms, filled with pieces of art on the walls and placed strategically on the floors. People were milling around holding glasses of champagne, talking in what sounded like appreciative hushed tones. She was looking for Luke when she saw her. That is, she saw herself, on the wall. She was asleep, in her own bedroom she recognised, legs curled up beneath her bottom, hands wrapped around her bump. Luke had painted it from that day, she realised. It was beautiful. Looking at the display card, it read LOVE SLEEPS, NOT FOR SALE.
Brushing away a tear, she felt a surge of hope and turned to find Luke. What she found was a perky pair of tits, attached to a very annoyed Victoria.
"And what are you doing here?" She enquired quietly, tapping her foot on the brilliant white floor. She put her arm around Cady and started to steer her to the entrance.
"This event is invitation only, it's not for ex-clients, so you have to leave, okay? I won't have you ruining Lukey's big night!"
Cady stopped in her tracks, causing the slighter than her Victoria to pitch forward.
Cady was not about to be ordered about anymore, and she was just in the mood for this one.
"Listen, Victoria is it, I came to speak to Luke, and speak to him I shall. I don't want to ruin his night, I just want to-"
Victoria again tried to steer her to the exit, but with Cady being the size of a small rotund bouncer these days, she didn't budge. "He can't see you here, you will ruin everything!" Victoria grunted with the effort of trying to move her. People were starting to stare

now, and Cady was defiant. She felt a dull ache in her back, but ignored it due to the even bigger pain in her arse.
Grabbing Victoria by the arm like a farmer would a chicken, she boomed, "Victoria, will you just PISS OFF!"
The whole room turned towards them now, and Victoria was red faced and in effect hanging in place by one spindly arm. The pair were just about to square up again when Luke appeared at the front of the gathering crowd. His face went from a slight double take of confusion, to lighting up at the sight of Cady, who at this moment like slightly like a wrestler on the winning side.
"Cady, you came? I am so - Victoria, will you do as she says please, and just piss off! I never wanted you to come here anyway."
Victoria's face was a picture as Cady released her arm and she dropped to the floor. Picking herself up, she glared at the pair and stamped from the room, knocking a waiter carrying champagne to the floor on the way past. The crowd dispersed, some picking up the waiter, and the pair was left alone. Cady rubbed her back and grimaced at the pain. Luke grabbed her other hand and stared at her with his beautiful big blue eyes.
"Cady, I am so glad.."
"No, let me speak please Luke," Cady shushed his full lips with her index finger.
"I really like you, Luke, I am sorry for how I acted, but I really would like you to be in my, our life. If that's alright with you." She looked at him hopefully, biting her lip, and he thought his heart would burst. "I love the painting of me, by the way," she smiled.
Luke grinned. "Wait till you see my apartment, it's like a shrine."
The pair giggled and Luke bent to kiss her. As his lips touched hers, she let out a shriek. Luke felt a gush of warm water hit his shoes and the pair looked at each, horror mirrored in their faces.
Luke grabbed her hands and whispered, "Cady, did your waters just break?"
She looked at him sheepishly, and then groaned as a contraction seized her stomach in a vice. Several people were looking now, and as Luke half carried, half helped her to the doors, they heard one person exclaim, "Wow, live art! This guy is amazing!"
They both sniggered and headed for Cady's car, puffing and panting all the way.

12 hours later, Cady was staring into the second pair of beautiful blue eyes she had seen that day, only these belonged to her daughter. A daughter that was perfect, and gorgeous, and here. Luke had been there throughout, mopping her brow and spurring her on, and he even cut the cord when Imogen was born. They both sat there, staring at this entirely new person, in a state of total euphoria.
Luke, sat on the bed next to his girls, bent his head and kissed them both.
"I need to go get changed and get the baby's things, will you be okay?"
Cady nodded, high on life. "Yes, and bring the car seat please? Priscilla and Dick will be here soon, that alright?"
Luke rolled his eyes. "They are her grandparents, I understand. And I think that Richard would have liked me, you know?"
She scrunched up her adorable nose at him. "You got something to tell me?"
He laughed. "Another day, sweetheart. I won't be long."
"Hurry back," she said, laughing as Imogen's mouth clamped onto her finger, rooting for food.
"Cady," Luke said softly. "Love you both."
She smiled and looked adoringly back at him.
"We love you too."

Richard's heart was fit to burst. Or it would be, if he still had a heart; he wasn't sure souls did. Gerty hugged him fiercely. "You did it child, you happy now?"
Richard nodded, tears in his eyes, throat thick with emotion. "I am yes, they will be okay, I know it."
Gerty smiled and straightened her robes.
"You ready to move on?" She held out her hand, just as one corner of the room opened up, showing a blinding, shimmering white light.
He took her hand, took one last look at Cady and Imogen and blew them a kiss.
"I'm ready."
And they walked into the light together.

When Luke called at his apartment to pack a bag full of clothes, he noticed someone had tinkered with his newest painting, a painting of Cady with a baby looking similar to Imogen in her arms.
Someone had written in paint at the bottom.
Never let her go..
Luke smiled and saluted the air.
“I promise, I never will.”

EPILOGUE

The sun was shining in Cady's garden as the buffet tables groaned with food. The Christening guests milled around, happy talk filling the air as they ate, drank and adored Imogen, who at four months old, was more stunning than ever. He had come home from the hospital with them that day, and had never left. His work was selling in spades now and he was a full time artist. She often teased him that it was her floor show that kick started his career. They had recently even started a project together, a children's picture book, and Cady had found that she loved her new work.

Luke was the perfect dad to Imogen and she adored him. He tickled her tummy as she sat in his lap, Cady looking on at the pair as Priscilla sat and chatted next to her. They were adoring grandparents and Cady was glad that they were so involved. They liked Luke and accepted that she was happy, and they had fallen into an easy relationship together.
Marcus and Angela had left the firm; after Luke and Cady had contacted him to tell him the truth, he had confronted her and she had confessed.
Marcus was devastated and had left to work at another firm, Cady had heard nothing from him since. As for the baby, she knew that Priscilla and Richard saw the child but it was something that she could never be cross at them for. It was a boy by all accounts, called Richard, and she wished the child well. Perhaps when the children were older, they could even meet and have a relationship, they were half brother and sister after all.

Looking across at George and Magda, she laughed as Magda fussed over the huge hunk of cheese that George was shovelling into her pregnant mouth. They were the best of friends now, and nothing had been heard from Ben. She was scheduled to take the baby to the States though to meet its grandparents, and Cady hoped that this trip would go well. Family was family, after all, no matter where it came from.
She gripped Luke's hand and he leaned into her, cradling the baby in his other arm.
"Are you okay, darling?"

Cady looked around her and back to Luke, their child snuggled against his chest.
"Luke, I can honestly say, I have a good life."

THE END

Dear Reader,

Thank you for taking the time to buy and read this book. I have many more romance stories available from bookshops and online retailers, and I love to hear from readers!

If you do get a chance, a review on Amazon and Goodreads really help authors to sell more books, and reach more readers. This means more books for you all!

I am on twitter @writerdove and Instagram @writerdove, or head over to my FB page Rachel Dove Author.

Happy reading everyone!

Rachel Dove

Made in the USA
Las Vegas, NV
24 March 2023